Praise for *Australia Day*

WINNER, VICTORIAN PREMIER'S LITERARY AWARD FOR FICTION, 2018

WINNER, VICTORIAN PREMIER'S LITERARY AWARD FOR AN UNPUBLISHED MANUSCRIPT, 2016

'Melanie Cheng is an astonishingly deft and incisive writer. With economy and elegance, she creates a dazzling mosaic of contemporary life, of how we live now. Hers is a compelling new voice in Australian literature.'

CHRISTOS TSIOLKAS

'What a wonderful book, a book with bite. These stories have a real edge to them. They are complex without being contrived, humanising, but never sentimental or cloying—and, ultimately, very moving.'

ALICE PUNG

'In each story, Melanie Cheng creates an entire microcosm, peeling back the superficial to expose the raw nerves of contemporary Australian society. Her eye is sharp and sympathetic, her characters flawed and funny and utterly believable.'

JENNIFER DOWN

'Melanie Cheng's stories are a deep dive into the diversity of humanity. They lead you into lives, into hearts, into unexplored places, and bring you back transformed.'

MICHELLE WRIGHT

T0363021

'The characters stay in the mind, their lives and experiences mirroring many of our own, challenging us to think how we might respond in their place. An insightful, sometimes uncomfortable portrayal of multicultural Australia from an observant and talented writer.'
RANJANA SRIVASTAVA

'Powerfully perceptive stories, written with love, humour, realism, and a distinct edginess. While the terrain covered might be familiar, Cheng's take on our treasured multiculturalism feels fresh…It's necessary reading, not only because it's a microcosm of who we are, but because each story is a gem.'
SIMON McDONALD

'Cheng's scientific training shows in her keen and dispassionate character observation. These no-fuss tales display a variety of people attending to their lives each wrapped snugly in their own skins and in their own heads but each curiously identifiable as Australian.'
SYDNEY MORNING HERALD

'A sumptuous collection.'
HERALD SUN

'If only the PM might pick up a copy, even by mistake.'
SATURDAY PAPER

'Cheng's work is polished and affecting. *Australia Day* is that thing we all chase: a complex, engaging and timely read.'
LIFTED BROW

'This smart, engaging short story collection offers fresh perspectives on what it means to be Australian today. The stories also explore identity and belonging in a variety of other ways, delving into family, love, class and education. Big themes aside, every story is beautifully written and a total pleasure to read.'

AUSTRALIAN WOMEN'S WEEKLY

'The author's empathetic eye and easy facility with dialogue make the anthology a strong debut, with the longer stories in particular offering breadth and depth.'

BIG ISSUE

'A bittersweet, beautifully crafted collection.'

BOOKS+PUBLISHING

'A stunning debut that takes its place among Australian short story greats…This is the kind of book you can read in one sitting, or space out one story a day to savour the experience.'

AU REVIEW

'The different cultures, the intriguing characters all left me wanting more. I'd love to see some longer fiction from Melanie Cheng in the future but I'll happily accept anything and everything she writes. A fantastic talent who has nailed the art of the short story.'

SAM STILL READING

Melanie Cheng is a writer and general practitioner. She was born in Adelaide, grew up in Hong Kong and now lives in Melbourne. Her debut collection of short stories, *Australia Day*, won the Victorian Premier's Literary Award for an Unpublished Manuscript in 2016 and the Victorian Premier's Literary Award for Fiction in 2018. Her first novel, *Room for a Stranger*, will be published by Text in 2019.

Australia Day

Melanie Cheng

TEXT PUBLISHING MELBOURNE AUSTRALIA

The Text Publishing Company acknowledges the Traditional Owners of the country on which we work, the Wurundjeri people of the Kulin Nation, and pays respect to their Elders past and present.

textpublishing.com.au

The Text Publishing Company
Wurundjeri Country, Level 6, Royal Bank Chambers, 287 Collins Street, Melbourne Victoria 3000 Australia

Copyright © Melanie Cheng, 2017

The moral right of Melanie Cheng to be identified as the author of this work has been asserted.

All rights reserved. Without limiting the rights under copyright above, no part of this publication shall be reproduced, stored in or introduced into a retrieval system, or transmitted in any form or by any means (electronic, mechanical, photocopying, recording or otherwise), without the prior permission of both the copyright owner and the publisher of this book.

This is a work of fiction. Names, characters, places and incidents are the product of the author's imagination. Any resemblance to actual persons, living or dead, is entirely coincidental.

First published by The Text Publishing Company, 2017
This edition published 2019
Reprinted 2021, 2022, 2023

Cover design by Sandy Cull, gogoGingko
Page design by Jessica Horrocks
Typeset by J&M Typesetting

Printed and bound in Australia by Griffin Press, a member of the Opus Group. The Opus Group is ISO/NZS 14001:2004 Environmental Management System certified.

National Library of Australia Cataloguing-in-Publication entry
Creator: Cheng, Melanie, author.
Title: Australia Day/by Melanie Cheng.
ISBN: 9781925603972 (paperback)
ISBN: 9781925410839 (ebook)
Subjects: Australia Day—Fiction. Short stories.

FSC
www.fsc.org
MIX
Paper | Supporting
responsible forestry
FSC® C018684

The paper this book is printed on is certified against the Forest Stewardship Council® Standards. Griffin Press, a member of the Opus Group, holds chain of custody certification SCS-COC-001185. FSC® promotes environmentally responsible, socially beneficial and economically viable management of the world's forests.

'There has never been a more exciting time to be an Australian.'

Prime Minister Malcolm Turnbull

To Mum, for feeding me books,
and Dad, for setting the bar high

Contents

Australia Day

The M1 is busy. Some vehicles—four-wheel drives and utes mainly—have Australian flags flying from their windows. Jess sits perfectly erect at the wheel, the same way she sits in lectures. A lamenting electropop hit is on the radio. The singer's howl cuts through the rattle of the 1987 Toyota Celica.

'Did you know that forty per cent of people who fly Australian flags would still support the White Australia policy?' Stanley asks when the song has finished.

The air conditioner is broken and beads of sweat catch in the hairs on Jessica's upper lip.

'Did you know that ninety per cent of statistics are made up on the spot?' she says.

'Saw it on the ABC.'

1

'Then it must be true.' Jess laughs. Her flaxen hair flaps against her cheeks. 'My dad has an Australian flag bumper sticker. What does that say about him?'

'The research looked at flags, not stickers. It would be wrong for me to extrapolate.'

A moth meets its messy demise on the windscreen. Powdered wings smear the glass.

'You're one of us now, remember? Got the native plant and everything.'

Stanley thinks of the once scarlet banksia plant, now draped in cobwebs on his balcony. Jess had come along for the citizenship ceremony. She'd worn a tangerine dress and dangly earrings.

'He's going to hate me, isn't he?' Stanley asks.

Jess waves a finger at the glove box. 'Pass me my sunnies.'

Stanley finds the glasses case beneath a packet of ribbed-for-her-pleasure condoms. Another one of Eddie's relics—lately Stanley has been unearthing them everywhere.

'Well?' he says.

Jess clears her throat. It is the first time, in two hours of driving, that Stanley has heard her cough.

'Deep down, Dad's just a big cuddly teddy bear.'

Eddie Mitchell studies medicine, like the rest of them. He is smart—he made the dean's honours list three years in a row—and good-looking (in a goofy, barefoot, Queensland

2

kind of way). Everybody loves him. Even Stanley, who is no match for that easy Sunshine Coast smile. If it weren't for Eddie, Stanley tells himself, he never would have found Jess that day at the anatomical pathology lab, bent over a glass box of dissected hands.

'Hi,' he'd said, all casual, as if sidling up to her at a bar.

'Piss off.'

'Stanley Chu. Nice to meet you.'

Jess ignored him. She examined the pool of mucus—a mixture of tears and snot—on the toilet paper in her palm. Stanley pulled up a stool. The metal legs made a grating noise across the linoleum floor. He sat down, and together they stared at the bodiless forearms, waving up at them from the box.

'Flexor pollicis longus,' Stanley said, pointing at a label pinned to one of the specimens. 'It should be flexor pollicis longus, not flexor carpi radialis.'

In tutes they were studying the neck and thorax. Jess had no idea about the upper limb.

'I've taken it up with my anatomy tutor,' he said. 'She's going to relabel it on Monday.'

Jess looked at Stanley's poreless skin and shiny almond-shaped eyes.

'Aren't you in my anatomy class?' she asked.

He blushed.

'You jiggle your leg on the stool.'

Stanley steadied his knee.

'It's annoying.' Jess shivered. Sun was pouring through the windows, but the laboratory felt unnaturally cool. 'How come you know upper limb already?'

'I got bored and read ahead.'

'Seriously? When I get bored I go for a coffee, or a bike ride. Something fun.'

'The brachial plexus is pretty extraordinary,' Stanley said, and his black eyes flashed wide. 'I could teach you about it sometime.' Stanley had memorised Jessica's student number. He knew that last semester, in anatomy, she had scraped by with 55. It was a passing grade, but only just.

Jessica said nothing.

'Red tits don't come back,' he said, and then, seeing the bewildered expression on her face, explained, 'It's a mnemonic: roots, trunks, divisions, cords, branches.'

'That's a relief. I wasn't sure what kind of tits you were talking about.'

They laughed. Stanley looked down at the macerated tissue in Jessica's hand.

'Why were you crying before?'

Jessica's smile evaporated. Everybody, including Stanley, knew that Eddie Mitchell had cheated on her with Stephanie Hubbard.

'It's not important.'

And in this cold glass room of formaldehyde-infused

body parts where a tit was a bird and nothing more, it wasn't.

A couple of heifers look up with mild interest as the crimson Celica rattles past. When the car reaches a letterbox fashioned from a milk can, Jess takes a sharp left turn. The hatchback splutters up the gravel driveway.

'I told you to get rid of that shitbox years ago!' Jessica's father bellows when they park in front of the house.

'Stanley,' Jess says, jumping out of the car, 'meet my dad. Dairy farmer and Ford Falcon tragic, Neville Cook.'

Neville sticks his pink, large-pored face up against the dusty glass. He grins. 'Pleased to meet you.'

Behind him stands an older version of Jessica—shorter and rounder but with the same broad, gap-toothed smile. She wears an apron, which reads *This hen cooks from scratch*, and has one arm around a long-haired teen.

Stanley gets out of the car as Jess slams her door shut.

'Let me look at you,' the woman says, letting go of the boy to grab her daughter with floury hands. She holds Jess at an arm's length and then, as if unable to bear the distance, pulls her into a tight embrace. 'Don't they feed you at these residential colleges? Never mind. We'll fatten you up. I've got your favourite, tuna casserole, in the oven. And apple pie for dessert.'

Stanley shifts his feet. His bladder is ready to burst. He'd looked respectable when they left Melbourne, but now his clothes are wet with sweat. Thankfully, nobody—except, perhaps, the oily teenager—takes much notice of him. They are too busy retrieving Jessica's duffel bag from the car and marvelling at the latest—*What is that? Strawberry blond?*—colour of her hair. It is really only when the family sits down to dinner that anybody remembers Stanley is there.

'When did the First Fleet arrive in Australia?'

'Twenty-sixth of January, seventeen eighty-eight.'

They were in Stanley's studio apartment on Spencer Street, swotting up for his citizenship test.

'I bet most *Australians*,' Jessica said, making quotation marks with her fingers, 'don't even know that.'

Stanley stood up and walked four paces to the kitchen—a corner with a hotplate and a couple of chipboard shelves.

'Tea?' he said as he flicked the switch on the kettle.

Jessica nodded.

He didn't understand the way Australians drank tea—the nurses in the hospital seemed to have made a religion of it, retreating every three hours to a dedicated 'tearoom' to cradle *World's Best Mum* mugs to their breasts. For Stanley, drinking tea was something done from porcelain cups, in restaurants, with family and friends.

'Do you miss it?' Jessica asked, pointing to a framed photo of him with his mother in the Tiger Balm gardens.

It was the wrong question. She should have asked: *What do you miss about it?* And then he would have answered: *The lights and the noise and the crowds and the chaos.* As it was, he only mumbled, 'Not really.'

'Beer?' Neville offers, pointing a crooked finger at Stanley.

Stanley nods. He has yet to develop a taste for beer—preferring spirits on the rare occasions that he does drink—but he doesn't want to appear rude.

'Would you like a glass?' Jessica's mother asks, pulling a tumbler from the dishwasher. Stanley looks around the table. Everybody is drinking beer, but not one of them is drinking from a glass.

'No thank you.'

Jessica's mother places a large ceramic dish in the middle of the table. Jessica's brother, who has not uttered a word since Stanley arrived, whispers, 'I hope you like tuna.'

'The British have a saying,' Stanley says, loudly, so everybody can hear, 'Chinese people eat everything with four legs…except the table.'

They all laugh, apart from the teenager, who points out that tuna fish don't have legs.

'Is that where you're from?' Mrs Cook asks, spooning a clump of macaroni and bechamel sauce onto Stanley's plate. 'China?'

'Hong Kong.'

Neville jumps in, his mouth bursting with pasta. 'Island or peninsula?'

Stanley wonders if he has underestimated Mr Cook. 'You know Hong Kong?'

'Pam and I paid a visit once,' Neville replies, clearly pleased with Stanley's reaction. 'Before we had kids.'

Pam wipes her hands on her apron. 'I bought a fake Rolex watch that still keeps perfect time.'

Stanley feels irrationally proud, as if he had assembled the cheap knock-off himself.

'They love all that stuff, don't they?' Neville goes on. 'Watches and cars and handbags.'

Stanley thinks of his cousin, Mei, who worked her summer holidays to buy a Chanel clutch.

'Stanley doesn't care about those things,' Jessica declares. 'Do you, Stanley.'

The entire family turns to look at him. Even Jessica's brother peeks through a gap in his fringe.

'Not really.'

'Another one, please, Pammy,' Neville says and bangs the butt of his beer bottle on the table. He turns to Stanley. 'They all want their kids to be doctors. The hotel doormen. The waiters. The taxi drivers. Everyone.'

Jessica locks eyes with Stanley, mouths an apology.

'I never pushed my kids into anything,' Neville says. 'I was hoping that one of them would want to take over the farm one day. But none of them did.' Pam replaces Neville's empty bottle with a fresh one. 'And look, that's okay. That's their choice in the end. And things change. I mean, who knows who Jess'll marry.' He takes a swig of his beer. 'If I'm lucky, he'll be an agriculture student with an interest in dairy farming. Stranger things have happened. And Rhys, well, when he grows up and realises art doesn't pay shit until you're dead—'

'Neville.' Pam shoots her husband a look. She turns to Stanley. 'Rhys did that beautiful landscape on the wall over there.'

A picture of the family home. The paint is laid on thick. Stanley knows nothing about art, but he likes the painting. He says so.

'You'll have to excuse my husband,' Pam says as she clears the plates. 'He's been in a foul mood ever since the Swans lost the grand final. Four months ago.'

'Dad's family were big South Melbourne fans,' Jess explains.

'And who do you barrack for, Stanley?' Pam asks.

Jessica beams. 'Stan's a North Melbourne man.'

Stanley freezes. He has never watched a game of football. He and his ex-housemate had only chosen the Kangaroos— for situations like this—back when they shared a townhouse in North Melbourne. *Doesn't matter which one you say*, his friend had said at the time, *as long as it's not Collingwood*.

9

But Neville isn't interested. Minutes pass. Stanley listens to the clink of forks on ceramic plates, the whirr of the fan in the oven. Jessica nudges his foot beneath the table. Pam stands up and walks to the stove. Finally Neville licks the last drop of beer from the mouth of his bottle.

'Hit me again, Pam.'

'How about dessert? I made Jess's favourite. Apple pie.' They all watch Pam pull the pastry from the oven. The smell of cooked apples and cinnamon fills the air.

Neville leans back in his chair. 'How about a drink with my slice of pie?'

Mrs Cook looks imploringly at Jess.

'How's the farm going, Dad?'

Neville keeps his flint-grey eyes firmly locked on his wife. 'Three dead from bloat last month.'

Stanley scrapes at his macaroni, which has hardened like industrial glue to his plate.

'Hello? Anyone home?' A timorous voice echoes down the hall.

'That'll be Linda,' Rhys says. 'Can I go?'

Mr Cook shifts his gaze to his son. 'Go on then.'

Rhys scrambles from the room.

'At least it's a girl,' Neville says when they hear Linda's car rumble down the hill.

*

After apple pie, Neville goes for a smoke. His large frame cuts an imposing silhouette against the battered flyscreen and purple sky.

'Jess, honey, why don't you take Stanley to his room?' Pam says. 'Let him settle in.'

Stanley follows Jessica down a long, dimly lit corridor. They pass a toilet that smells of lavender, and then Rhys's room with its hanging yellow road sign, before Jess throws open the door to her old bedroom.

'Hope you don't mind,' she says.

Stanley doesn't mind—it is spacious and clean—but he is a little surprised. The Jessica he knows doesn't quite match the rose-coloured quilt and neat row of teddy bears propped against the pillow.

'Mum's a hoarder,' Jess explains. 'She keeps absolutely everything.'

Stanley kicks off his shoes and throws his backpack onto the mattress. A yellow bear in a waistcoat falls onto the floor at Jessica's feet.

'It's perfect,' Stanley says.

Jessica picks up the bear and straightens its vest before placing it on the dresser. 'There's a fresh towel on the chair.'

Stanley collapses onto the bed. Springs, arthritic from disuse, groan beneath his bottom. Jessica puts her hand on the brass doorknob. Without turning around, she says, 'I'm really sorry, Stanley. About Dad.'

She never calls him Stanley. He is, and always has been, Stan. Sometimes even *Stan the man*.

'That's okay,' he says, his thoughts turning, for some reason, to the citizenship test. He thinks how much better it would be if it included scenarios just like this one.

When faced with an awkward situation while visiting the parents of your Australian friend (who is not yet your girlfriend but who you hope, some day, might be), the most appropriate response would be:

A) Apologise—because, after all, it is always your fault.

B) Empathise—e.g., 'This must be really hard for you.'

C) Stand up for yourself—e.g., 'I don't have to put up with this.'

D) Brush it off—e.g., 'No worries, mate.'

After a moment of deep thought, Stanley opts for D.

The room smells of dust and mildew and naphthalene balls. Around eleven, Stanley hears whispers in the hall.

'So?'

Jess.

'He's *sweet*.'

And Mrs Cook.

'Isn't he?'

'But—'

A groan of pipes. Rushing water.

'But what?'

Buzz of an electric toothbrush. Spitting. Squeak of a rusty tap.

'He's no Eddie.'

A patter of slippered feet. Click of a light switch. The thump of doors being pulled firmly closed.

Stanley had tried to talk to his mother about Jess, once. It was a Sunday night and she'd called him at the usual time of eight o'clock—in the half-hour window between dinner and the start of her favourite soap opera.

'Have you eaten yet?' she said. A standard Cantonese greeting.

'Yes.' He could hear the tinny sound of the TV, ads for watches and anti-dandruff shampoo. 'Where's Dad?'

'Out.' His mother's euphemism for gambling. She would wait up for him tonight, on the couch, as she munched on dried watermelon seeds.

'Ma.'

'What? Is something the matter?'

Stanley imagined coming straight out and saying it, like some American son in the movies. *I've met someone.* He pictured the fallout. *Is she Chinese? What does her father do?*

'Nothing's wrong. I have a new study partner, that's all.'

'Study partner,' his mother scoffed, before blowing her

nose into the phone. 'That's the problem with Australians. They think everybody's equal. You can't study in groups. Everybody's at different levels.'

Stanley scratched big circles onto an old gas bill with a biro. 'You're right.'

'And you should call your grandma.'

'Why? Is everything okay?'

'You need to apologise.'

'For what?'

'For never calling.'

Sleep evades him. Five years ago, when Stanley had first arrived in Australia, he'd downloaded albums of traffic noise from the iTunes store. Now, in the impenetrable blackness of the bush, he finds his earphones and plugs himself in. As he listens, he pictures himself back on the balcony of his parents' Mong Kok apartment, perched on a plastic stool between a sagging clothesline and a dripping air conditioning unit. He imagines himself looking up at a sky that is not flat and blue and interminable, but choked with smog and cut into neat slices by the blades of the buildings.

At three am Jessica sneaks into his room.

'I can't sleep,' she says before sliding into the bed. She slips her fingers inside his T-shirt. Stanley feels her hot breath on the back of his neck.

'Me neither.' He doesn't turn around to face her. He doesn't want her to know about his body's dramatic, involuntary response to her presence in his bed. Instead they lie, curled together, facing the wall.

'I never knew you were a teddy bear kind of girl.'

'Shut up.' Jess play-punches him on the shoulder.

'I hope this bed has seen more teddy bears than boys.'

Jess laughs. 'Dad made sure of that.'

'Your dad's scary. He should get a job at Guantanamo Bay.' Jessica says nothing, but Stanley feels her body stiffen beside him. 'I'm joking.' Talk of Neville is enough to make Stanley lose his erection. He rolls to face his friend and runs his fingertips across her lips in the dark. 'I like this.'

Jessica buries her face in Stanley's shoulder. Her hair smells of sweat and shampoo and apple pie. Stanley wonders if she can hear his heart doing somersaults behind his sternum. If she can, she says nothing. Within minutes he hears heavy breathing, quickly followed by a soft snore.

When Stanley opens his eyes the next morning, Jess is gone. For a moment he wonders if he imagined the whole thing, but then he discovers one of Jessica's earrings buried beneath the doona. He stuffs the earring inside his backpack. Even though nothing happened, he doesn't want Neville finding any evidence of Jessica sharing his bed.

Stanley peers through a gap in the curtain. The entire

Cook family is outside his window, cleaning the barbecue and filling an esky with beer. He takes advantage of the momentary privacy inside the house to brush his teeth, shower and dress. There is no lock on the bathroom door, only a sign with a picture of roses, which says *Patience is a virtue.*

Once clean, he goes outside to look for Jess. He finds her with her father, beside the barbecue, counting sausages.

'How many people are coming again?' Stanley hears Jessica ask.

'Around twenty, give or take.'

Stanley's heart sinks. Jessica had given him the impression it would just be a family thing.

'Morning, sleepyhead!' Jessica calls when she sees him.

Stanley feels his cheeks burn.

'Must be all that beer from last night!' Neville jeers.

'Be nice, Daddy,' Jess says and waves a pair of heavy tongs at her father.

'Your dad's right,' Stanley says. 'Chinese people lack a specific enzyme for metabolising alcohol.'

'Exactly.' Jessica places a sympathetic hand on Stanley's shoulder and looks at her father. 'He can't help it.'

What's left of the morning is spent preparing for lunch. Pam makes an enormous batch of potato salad. Neville appraises the piles of meat. Jessica marinates the chicken wings. Stanley hovers, arranging sauce bottles in a straight line on the table. At midday, the first guest arrives—a short, barrel-chested man with grey sideburns and laughing eyes. Jessica introduces Stanley as her good friend from uni. The man shakes Stanley's hand. When he finds out Stanley is a medical student, he launches into a detailed account of his wife's battle with pancreatic cancer—a story, he says, that Jessica has heard a thousand times.

Minutes later, a ute and two four-wheel drives storm up the driveway. Family friends pour out of the vehicles, carrying desserts and six-packs of beer. Jessica, away for so long in the city, is the unofficial guest of honour. She rolls her eyes when nobody is looking to show Stanley she hasn't forgotten him, which makes him almost content to sit on a plastic chair next to the speakers with Rhys. After twenty minutes, Rhys leans into the esky beside him and pulls out a cold beer. He passes it to Stanley.

'Thanks,' Stanley says, not daring to rebuff what he imagines is a rare gesture of kindness. For another twenty minutes they sit in silence, watching the group and taking swigs from their bottles.

'I hate Australia Day,' Rhys says, finally, before cracking open another Carlton Draught.

Aside from the citizenship ceremony, today is the first time Stanley has celebrated it. He nods.

'Bunch of nostalgic bullshit,' Rhys says. Then, sensing he

might have offended Stanley, he adds, 'Thanks for saying you liked my painting.'

Stanley can feel the alcohol in his cheeks, his hands, his feet. He resists the urge to scratch. 'No worries.'

He is saved from any further awkward questions by the late arrival of another guest. Stanley recognises the Toyota Tarago straight away. When Eddie Mitchell emerges from the van, the throng immediately makes way for him. As Eddie walks up, Neville yells his name and gives him a loud slap across the shoulder. Jessica is no longer the centre of attention. Everybody is watching Eddie. Everybody except Rhys, who is watching Stanley.

'Happy Australia Day,' Rhys says and raises his beer.

The rest of the afternoon is a blur. When Linda arrives, Rhys disappears with her inside the house, leaving Stanley alone on a camp chair under a tree. He drinks two more beers in quick succession until his head is swimming. Only Mrs Cook seems concerned about his welfare, stopping every half-hour to talk and to offer him a plate of food. Chicken wings and potato salad. A sausage with sauce on white bread. Pineapple cooked on the barbecue with a large mound of vanilla ice-cream.

As Stanley eats, he watches Eddie. Jessica's ex-boyfriend has not dressed up for the occasion: he is wearing a T-shirt with a hole in the shoulder and faded board shorts. Everybody wants a piece of him. As soon as he finishes talking to one person, another partygoer sidles in. Stanley wonders who invited him. He suspects Neville, but really it could be any of them. Even Jessica. It's clear that she's still in love with Eddie from the way she drifts around him—pretending to ignore him but laughing loudly and never quite letting him out of her sight. It is only once Eddie disappears to the toilet, late in the afternoon, that she goes in search of Stanley.

'I'm sorry,' she says when she finally finds him. But she doesn't clarify what she is sorry for. It could be anything: her invasion of his bed last night, inviting Eddie, the way she's ignored him the entire day.

All the silent watching has made Stanley angry. 'Did you know he was coming?'

'Of course not,' Jess says, but she won't make eye contact with him. 'We were together for two years—I guess he became part of the family.'

'And they still accept him, after what he did?'

'I told them when we broke up it was a mutual thing.'

Stanley thinks back to that day in the anatomical pathology lab. How desperately he had wanted to make Jessica smile, how delighted he was when she did.

'He's broken up with Stephanie.'

Stanley's head pounds. 'How convenient for you.'

'What's that supposed to mean?'

Stanley feels two hands pressing down on his shoulders like sandbags. It's Eddie.

'Lover's tiff?' Eddie jokes. He lets go of Stanley and sits down on Rhys's empty camp chair.

'Shut up,' Jessica says, with the same tone of feigned annoyance she used with Stanley the night before.

Stanley examines Eddie, takes in his eager-to-please eyes, his dopey smile. For once Stanley feels a kinship with the guy. Then he looks at Jessica, the girl responsible for bringing them here, to the middle of nowhere. There is a cluster of pimples on her forehead and the first blush of sunburn across her nose. When she leans into the esky, Stanley catches a glimpse of the tattoo on her lower back—the Chinese character for double happiness, written crudely, as if by a child.

When they head back to Melbourne the next day, Stanley insists on driving. It feels good to grip the wheel with both hands and steer the car down the gravel driveway. Stanley's headache is gone, but the sunlight is intolerable. Jessica lends him her sunglasses. At the halfway point, they stop to fill up the car with petrol and grab a Big Mac meal from McDonald's. Jess feeds Stanley French fries as they speed down the freeway towards the city. They don't speak. They only stare through the windshield at the straight black road and the clear blue sky and the occasional bright yellow hazard signs.

Big Problems

The Simpson Desert rippled like an orange sea through the cabin window. It was just as Leila had imagined—hot, callused, other-worldly. Like Mars. She leant back in her seat, sipped a plastic cup of red wine. It was a relief to be in the air, away from Melbourne and the Kelly family. Not that the Kelly family hadn't been good to her. They had been more than good, paying her double the recommended hourly rate and installing a smart TV, complete with Netflix, in her spacious bedroom. Even the twins, Orlando and Olivia, were well behaved and mature. Nothing like some of the horror stories she had read on the online forums. Leila was relieved, and grateful. But Alison and James could be suffocating. While they scorned helicopter parents—the twins loved to boast about riding on motos, helmetless, in Cambodia—with Leila, the Kellys were overprotective. Leila put this down to their guilt about employing an au pair. Hiring people to look after your children wasn't common in Australia. Mothers still prided themselves on being able to work *and* cook fresh meals *and* make costumes for the school play, even if it meant they wore a permanently frazzled look and occasionally forgot to pick up their least favourite child from school.

Leila presumed the Kellys had chosen her, with her Syrian background, as a means of alleviating some of this guilt. She knew it was a risk, mentioning her background on the au pair website, but she also thought it was a good way of vetting Islamophobes. And it had worked. The Kellys embraced Leila's heritage. Alison, the mother, was always probing Leila about what Syria was like, before the war had destroyed it. But Leila couldn't tell her. She had been born and raised in London. This seemed a constant source of disappointment to Mrs Kelly.

The Kellys were good people. James was the CEO of a not-for-profit organisation and Alison worked for Legal Aid. Though the kids could be precocious—Orlando wanted to be a human rights lawyer and Olivia described herself as an atheist—for the most part, they did as they were told. Even so, when James informed Leila they would be travelling to Bangkok for the school holidays and wouldn't need her on the trip, Leila found herself fantasising about the sleep-ins, the long hot baths and the silence she would enjoy. Even this plane trip seemed gloriously civilised compared to her day job. She could think in peace without an eleven-year-old asking her yet another question she couldn't answer.

Leila leant her head against the window. Clouds cast crisp black shadows across the fissured earth below. She took a photo through the glass to send to her mother once she landed. For years, Leila's mum had talked about visiting Australia, but the island continent with its mammoth sky and boundless beaches had always seemed a long way from home.

A man in an akubra hat was waiting for Leila in the arrivals hall. The twins had versed her in all things outback before she departed Melbourne—akubra hats, king brown snakes, bush flies, feral camels. The man held a handwritten sign with her name on it: *Leila Ayers*. The Kellys had insisted on paying for her to join a tour, which was strange, given they often boasted about their off-the-beaten-track travel. It filled Leila with an odd combination of annoyance and relief. Though desperate to assert her independence, she had seen the movie *Wolf Creek* too.

'Welcome to Alice Springs,' the man in the akubra hat said. He was ruddy-faced with hands like slabs of meat. 'Just waiting on a couple of others.'

Leila nodded and put on her sunglasses. Even in the

shelter of the arrival hall the light was unforgiving. She looked around, taking in the flame-red Qantas signs and the carpet with its undulating ochre design. She looked down at a backpacker, resting on a pile of bags on the floor. Leila had never travelled by herself before. After A levels, she and her friends had gone to Paris for a long weekend, but they were a large group of girls and had safety in numbers.

Akubra-hat-man changed the sign to one that read *Mr and Mrs Brown*. Almost immediately, a brightly dressed couple materialised at the baggage carousel. The man wore a baseball cap, and the woman a plastic visor. Even before they spoke, Leila knew they were American.

'Harry and Cynthia Brown. From Charlottesville, Virginia,' the man said, thrusting out his hand.

'Leila Ayers,' she replied. 'From London.'

They followed the driver to a dusty four-wheel drive in the airport car park. As they drove, the Americans told the man in the akubra hat about their travels. They listed the names of places Leila had never heard of: Cradle Mountain, Birdsville, Broome, Rottnest Island. She listened to their descriptions of beaches and glacial lakes as she stared out her grimy window. Looking at the red earth and spiny plants, it was hard to believe they were talking about the same country.

As they neared the town centre, Leila watched a brown-skinned boy with straw-coloured hair ride a battered bike on the road beside them. He bent his head and pedalled furiously, but he could not keep up with the bus. Minutes later she saw a woman asleep on a mattress laid straight onto the bare earth. The woman was wearing a cardigan in spite of the heat, and a mangy dog was licking her feet. Suddenly the world Leila had inhabited for the past three months— one of skinny lattes and children's yoga and organic bakeries where a loaf of bread cost seven dollars—seemed obscene.

Akubra-hat-man, whose name was Max, dropped Leila at her hostel. The Americans had climbed out first at a fancy resort called Palm Springs. 'Pick you up at six!' she heard Max yell as he disappeared in a cloud of dust. Leila looked up at the two-storey building. It was rectangular and ugly and painted a garish mauve. There was a campervan parked out the front with graffiti on the rear window: *Life sux if your girlfriend doesn't.* The dreadlocked man at reception, another Brit, gave Leila the key to her room. 'Let me know if you want company,' he said, his smile revealing a gold tooth.

She left the reception area and walked past the pool— a shallow above-ground structure with a few broken deckchairs around its edge. A girl in a polka-dot swimsuit was lying on a towel listening to music.

The room was clean enough. There was a single bed, and a small TV mounted to one of the walls. The only window opened onto a concrete courtyard with a plastic table and a barbecue. The air was thick with the smell of sausages. Leila could hear two men talking loudly about full moon parties in Thailand. One was bragging about buying 'diet pills', which were actually ecstasy, from the local pharmacy. The other was reminiscing about an Israeli dive instructor who had a mouth like Scarlett Johansson.

Leila sat down on the bed and pulled out her itinerary.

Day 1: Depart Alice Springs for Uluru (Ayers Rock)

Day 2: Uluru—Kata Tjuta National Park

Day 3: Uluru (Ayers Rock) to Watarrka (Kings Canyon)

Day 4: Depart Kings Canyon for Alice Springs

Leila wondered if her father's family had common ancestry with the man the rock was named after. She hoped not. She didn't fancy the idea of people going around stamping their names on things.

She peeked through the dusty curtain. In the courtyard, a group of girls in string bikinis had joined the men. One of the girls had brought a speaker down from her room. Now the shrieks and giggles were accompanied by a booming bass. Leila contemplated joining them, but the very thought made her heart race. She was not good in groups. Often she spent minutes perfecting a story in her head only to find that by the time she was ready to tell it, the conversation had moved on. She ate a muesli bar for dinner and read a book on Aboriginal history she had borrowed from the Kellys' library instead.

Hours passed. She read about songlines—routes taken

by Indigenous people's ancestral beings as they created everything in the natural world. She learnt about the storytelling tradition common to Aboriginal cultures— how information is passed from generation to generation through dance and spoken word and song. She discovered that Dreaming stories were not only intricate maps of the country but complex lessons in ethics and morality. As she read, she tried to block out the sound of a couple having loud sex in the room next door.

There were ten people on the tour, including Leila—the Americans she had met at the airport, a white woman from South Africa who had recently moved to the Sunshine Coast, two middle-aged sisters from Italy who didn't speak much English and an Australian family with young children— a boy and girl—from Sydney. Not one person on the trip was aged within ten years of Leila. She plugged herself into her phone and slept throughout the six-hour drive to Uluru.

Apart from the American couple, everybody was staying in cabins at the camping ground. Meals were included. The first night was an all-you-can-eat, meet-and-greet barbecue. Leila picked up a plate and joined the winding queue. She was soon found by the South African lady, who had changed into knee-length shorts and Birkenstock sandals. A gold cross nestled in the speckled cleavage between her breasts.

'You said you were from London?' the woman asked.

'Yes.'

They moved forward in the line.

'I'm Ellen.'

'Leila.'

Ellen spooned some potato salad onto her plate. 'Do you have family in Australia?'

'No.' Leila thought it an odd question, as if everyone from England should have relatives in the former colony. 'I'm working in Melbourne. As an au pair.'

Ellen picked up a burnt sausage with a pair of tongs. Without asking, she placed it on Leila's plate. 'I had a nanny in South Africa.'

Leila imagined a large black woman with a white bonnet and frilly apron.

'The kids *still* talk about her.'

Leila walked to an empty table and Ellen followed her. There was a group of Japanese tourists at the table beside them spraying themselves with insect repellent.

Ellen groaned as she sat down. 'Arthritis,' she explained and rubbed her knees with her hands. 'So what do you think of Australia?'

Leila flicked an ant off the summit of her potato salad. 'It's nice. The people are friendly.'

'It's a lucky country.'

Leila thought of the beaches along Port Phillip Bay and the sun and the Kellys' four-bedroom bungalow. She nodded.

'The blacks only make up three per cent of the population.'
Leila stopped nodding.

'Back home in South Africa we have big problems.' Ellen
wiped some tomato sauce from her lips with her napkin. 'Big
problems.'

Leila chewed on the burnt sausage, which suddenly felt
like broken sticks of charcoal in her mouth.

Leila had always been able to pass for white. Much to her
disappointment, she had not inherited her mother's lush
black eyelashes or coppery skin. As a baby, she'd had blond
hair, and her brown eyes had a splash of green in them.
Only her name, Leila, hinted at her Arabic roots, and even
that had become mainstream. Apart from Mrs Kelly, Leila
couldn't remember a single person ever asking about her
background.

Leila's mother, on the other hand, was a loud and proud
Syrian. If people didn't enquire about her heritage, it wasn't
long before she told them. People often mistook her for
Spanish or South American. On those occasions, Leila felt
sorry for the check-out chick or hairdresser or bank teller
who had made the error, because they would then have to
endure a short lesson on Syrian history. Leila's mother loved
to tell people how the capital, Damascus, was one of the
oldest continually inhabited cities in the world.

*

It was five-thirty in the morning. The bus had pulled over by the side of the road for the tourists to watch the sun rise over Uluru. The desert was cold and dark. Max, the tour guide, handed out blankets and mugs of freshly brewed coffee. The Italian sisters, keen photographers, cleaned their camera lenses and assembled their tripods. The Australian family and the American couple were deep in discussion about whether or not to climb the rock.

'I would,' Ellen interjected, 'if not for the arthritis in my knees.'

They had all seen the sign.

'WE DON'T CLIMB'
OUR TRADITIONAL LAW TEACHES US
THE PROPER WAY TO BEHAVE.
WE ASK YOU TO RESPECT OUR LAW BY
NOT CLIMBING ULURU.

It was a polite appeal to visitors by the traditional owners of the land. But the climb was not prohibited, except on windy days, and today was not a windy day.

Leila walked away from the group. She crossed the road, put her earbuds in. In the dark, the rock was just a shadow, but even its shadow was colossal, like the silhouette of a beast asleep on the smooth black land. Soon the sun peered across the rock's shoulders, momentarily blinding them all. When they finally regained their sight, they saw the beast's muscles stretch and flex beneath a dome of light.

Leila and the others watched the climbers, reduced to the size of ants against the hulk of the rock, as they waited for the start of the tour. Leila tried to pick the three tiny dots that were the American couple and the Australian father.

'Minga!' a voice boomed from behind the group. Leila, Ellen and the Italian sisters stopped looking up at the rock and turned towards the speaker. He was a tall Aboriginal man with green eyes and a wide-brimmed black hat.

'That's what we call the climbers in our language.' He pointed a finger at the rock. 'See that white line?'

Leila looked at the chalky streak on the rock's orange face.

'That's the mark left by people's footprints.'

'Like a scar,' Leila said.

Ellen glared at her.

The man smiled. 'Name's Jimmy,' he said, tipping his hat. 'I'll be your guide around Uluru today.'

As they walked, Jimmy told them how his ancestors had lived in the caves at Uluru, feeding on grains, honey ants and bush raisins. He told them the story of Kuniya, the sand python. He tried to explain Tjukurpa to them. He told them how Tjukurpa was law, teaching people how to care for one another and the land around them.

'It's the past, the present and the future all at once,' he said.

*

When they arrived back at the start of their walk, two hours later, they saw a large group gathered around an ambulance. The Sydney mother sprinted towards the crowd shouting loudly for Tim. Leila presumed that was her husband's name. The children didn't move but stayed with the group, watching their mother with glassy eyes. Ellen, who was closest, kneeled down and gathered the children to her, pushing their faces into the two enormous pillows of her breasts. Luckily Tim soon emerged, with his wife, tall and unscathed. The children ran towards him.

It turned out it was Harry Brown who was responsible for all the commotion. He'd had an attack of angina halfway up the rock. There had been two doctors on the climb with him, an anaesthetist from Canada and a cardiologist from Germany, and they had escorted him back down. Cynthia Brown had almost fainted with the excitement of it all, and she and her husband were rushed to the medical centre at Ayers Rock Resort.

It was a smaller and more sombre group that climbed back on the bus at four o'clock. The early-morning start and the heat had taken their toll. The Sydney mother wore an annoyed I-told-you-so face, and the children, sensing something was up, played quietly on their iPads. Even the Italian sisters, who were always calm, looked less relaxed than usual. Max tried to lighten the mood with a couple of inappropriate jokes about Yankees and sand pythons, but it was no use—the tourists refused to be moved.

As they drove back to the resort, Leila's thoughts turned to her English grandfather. Like Mr Brown, he had suffered from angina, and Leila knew what a serious condition it could be. He used to say it felt like a tired old elephant had decided to take a rest on his chest. It was an image that had appealed to five-year-old Leila. For years afterward, whenever she saw her pa, she imagined a weary elephant trailing behind him.

Leila was close to her father's parents, Nan and Pa, but she had only met her Syrian grandparents once. She was just three at the time, but the journey was such a novelty, the memories had been seared into her brain. French doors with paint peeling in long white ribbons. Cream tiles with flecks of gold, cool to the touch of her toes. Coffee brewing in a copper pot on the hot blue tongues flickering up from the stove. Most of all she remembered the light—a glow neither watery like the British sun, nor hot and white like the Australian one. It had warmed Leila from the inside out. Like tea. Familiar, somehow.

Harry Brown was in a stable condition at Alice Springs Hospital—at least that's what Max told them once they had got back to Alice Springs themselves. Two full days had passed since the incident at Uluru. Leila had almost forgotten about the Browns during a swim in the 'Garden of Eden' at Kings Canyon. As she lay floating in the waterhole, staring up at the patch of cloudless sky between the walls of orange rock, the fate of any individual—Harry Brown or otherwise—had seemed irrelevant.

It was the last night of the four-day tour, and the group had gathered in a small theatre in Todd Mall, the town's main shopping precinct. Leila was perched on a plastic seat, flanked by Tim and Ellen. The Italian sisters were sitting silently in the row immediately behind them. There were still a few minutes before the cultural extravaganza started.

'Lucy's back at the hotel with the kids,' Tim said, excusing his wife's absence. 'They're buggered.'

Leila hadn't seen the Australian couple speak directly to each other since they left Uluru. They communicated through their children instead. *Ask Daddy to take a photo of us. Tell Mummy you're hungry.*

'She still upset about Ayers Rock?' Ellen said, ignoring Tim's clear desire to avoid the subject.

'She'll get over it.'

'Wives worry about their husbands,' Ellen replied solemnly. 'It's normal.'

Tim shook his head. 'She thought it was disrespectful. To the traditional owners.' Now that the issue had been broached, he seemed relieved to be speaking about it.

34

'Big problems,' Ellen said, shaking her head. 'We've got big problems back home in South Africa.' She looked behind, at the Italians. 'But it's not just Africa. Look at Europe!' The sisters, surprised that they were suddenly being included in the conversation, simply nodded. 'And not just Europe!' Ellen said. 'England too!'

They all turned to look at Leila.

Leila felt a rush of blood, hot and itchy, to her chest and neck. 'Yes,' she agreed, gripping the edge of her seat. 'But I'm probably not the best person to ask. Mum being Syrian and everything.'

The room was thrust into darkness. On the stage a lone spotlight shone on an Aboriginal man with a didjeridu. Lines of white paint fell in diagonals across the man's pulsating cheeks. Leila felt the thrum, like a cat's purr, through the soles of her feet. For a moment it was as if the entire world were vibrating, not just the tiny theatre in Todd Mall. Leila imagined her mother, sipping a cup of tea in England, trembling with the music too.

Macca

The community health centre is sandwiched between a laundromat and a 7-Eleven. Dr Garrett sits in the windowless tearoom alone, drinking her coffee. She doesn't want to read the only magazine—a *Reader's Digest* from 2012—so she reads the laminated signs above the sink instead. *One soaker leads to many soakers! Don't put empty cartons of milk back into the fridge! If the dishwasher is full of clean dishes, EMPTY IT!* She imagines an army of people in aprons and rubber gloves shouting at her all at once.

When she has finished, she walks back down the narrow corridor towards the reception area. Her consulting room still smells faintly of the feet of the homeless man she saw before lunch. She sprays a few puffs of the air freshener she keeps in the top drawer of her desk. Her one o'clock has arrived. His name is Patrick MacCarthy and he has been waiting for 9 minutes, 12 seconds. She browses Mr MacCarthy's past medical history. Forty-nine. Stage 1 melanoma. Untreated hypertension. Smoker of 30 to 50 cigarettes per day. She hopes to God he is here today for something simple. A blood pressure check, perhaps, or a prescription for an antifungal. She is not in the mood for emotional excavation, financial strife, domestic violence or depression. She wants to give Mr MacCarthy what he wants and send him on his merry way.

The only man in the waiting room looks older than forty-nine. His face is scored with deep lines—dark, seemingly bottomless fissures, like those on an ancient rock face. Dr Garrett can just see the outline of the skin graft on his cheek—an island of smooth pink skin—where the melanoma was removed ten years ago.

'My name is Dr Garrett, but you can call me Emily.'

'Macca,' he says, sitting down and fiddling with the crotch of his tracksuit pants. 'Me daughter's name is Emily.'

Dr Garrett is surprised. She would have predicted something less traditional. Something like Shayna or Janelle.

'Her favourite things are Lady Gaga and spaghetti bolognese.'

Dr Garrett uncrosses her legs, plants her feet firmly beneath the desk. 'What can I do for you today?'

'Court ordered me to come.'

'The court ordered you? To see me?'

'Not you pacifically.' Macca makes broad strokes in the air with his heavily tattooed arms. 'This place.'

'Right.' Dr Garrett types the words *court order* into Macca's electronic file. She hesitates before swivelling back to face him again.

'Well, then, Macca, what does the court want me to do for you today?'

'Get me off the grog.' He grins. She sees that he is missing a top left incisor.

'And do you see your drinking as a problem?'

'I don't want to go to jail, if that's what you're getting at.'

But that is not what Dr Garrett is getting at. She wishes to God she knew what she was getting at.

'I've got me kid to think about. And me missus.'

He reaches for his cigarettes but stops himself when he remembers where he is.

'You're married,' she says.

'Separated.'

She adds this detail to the social history section of Macca's file.

'But we're working on it.' He clears his throat. 'For Emily.'

Dr Garrett waits for a respectful amount of time to pass—roughly ten seconds—before continuing.

'And do you mind me asking where you're living at the moment?'

She sees Macca eye the shiny bag with its silver buckle tucked beneath her desk.

'On me brother's floor. Just until I get me shit together. You know how it is.'

She looks up, and for a moment, the briefest of moments, their eyes meet across the messy desk.

'And your brother,' she says, turning back to face the computer screen. 'Does he drink?'

'Hammer?' Macca says and laughs as if his brother's drinking habits should be public knowledge. 'Like a fish.'

Dr Garrett stays behind after the clinic has closed to complete her paperwork. At five-thirty the receptionist calls to ask her how much longer she will be.

'Five minutes.'

She blames Macca. He threw a spanner into what might otherwise have been an unremarkable day. As it was, she'd ended up running forty-five minutes late. Mrs Weatherington was unhappy because she'd missed her midafternoon snack, and being diabetic—as she liked to point out repeatedly to anyone who would listen—a cheese sandwich was all that was standing between her and a hypoglycaemic coma.

'You right?'

She looks up to see Jeff's smiling red face in the doorway.

'Just shutting down now.'

Jeff is the most senior doctor in the practice. Emily likes

him. He is one of those country-trained GPs who could treat a cow for bloat and deliver a baby in the same day.

'You know, Em,' he says, taking a seat in the patient chair. 'This afternoon, as I sat listening to a morbidly obese woman tell me how she really only ever eats salads and how her husband left her for a younger and skinnier version of herself and how this has made her eat more, even though, really, what she eats is hardly anything at all...'

Emily laughs.

'I found myself getting sucked into her black hole of helplessness and negativity.'

The computer expires with a melodious sigh.

'And as I sat there, half-listening, half-trying to devise solutions to her insoluble problems, it hit me. Like Newton's apple. None of this was my problem.'

Dr Garrett thinks this a little harsh.

'It was a revelation. They were her problems, not mine. Not ours. Not yours.' Jeff slaps his hand emphatically on the edge of her desk. 'You should remind yourself of that, Emily. You should say it to yourself at the beginning and the end of every day. Help the poor buggers as much as you can within the confines of this room, but whatever you do, don't take their shit home with you.'

'Okay.'

'Remember that.'

'I will.'

'Not your problem.'

'Right.'

'Say it.'

'Not my problem.'

'Amen.'

He looks different today. Dr Garrett can't quite put her finger on it—a haircut, perhaps, or a clean shave—but he seems younger, sprightlier, less sedate. When she calls him from the waiting room, he hurries at her heels like a toddler, bubbling with unspoken words.

'I've been thinking a lot lately, about what you said.'

'What I said?'

'If I thought me drinking was a problem.'

'You said you didn't want to go to prison if you could help it.'

'Yeah, well...' He examines his freshly cut fingernails. 'That was a cop-out.'

Macca leans across the desk. It is a sudden movement that takes Dr Garrett by surprise. She can see every line in his corrugated face, feel every puff of his coffee-cigarette breath on her cheek. Her fingers find the duress alarm—two big red keys—hidden beneath her desk. She lets her hand hover there as she waits for him to speak.

'Let's do it.'

*

The drug and alcohol worker's name is Rowena, but she prefers to be called Ro. She could be beautiful if she wanted to be, but she doesn't want to be and so she is not. She has short hair, dyed a lifeless black, and a cold sore on her top lip. She wears a Pink Floyd *Dark Side of the Moon* T-shirt and a leather band on her left wrist.

'All inpatient beds are taken,' she says, licking milk froth from the edge of her coffee cup. 'Our only option is home detox.'

Dr Garrett summarises Macca's history as Rowena scribbles in her notebook. *Court order. Twelve beers a day. Old track marks left arm.* It is agreed. Dr Garrett will prescribe small quantities of diazepam for Macca to pick up from the chemist every couple of days. Hammer will dispense these to Macca as required to keep the tremors at bay. Rowena will do a home visit on day two—the point at which the more severe symptoms, like hallucinations, can kick in—to see how he is getting on. She will be contactable by mobile phone twenty-four hours a day. Dr Garrett will review Macca's progress back at the clinic the following week.

They have a plan. It may have been crudely constructed—getting the notorious binge drinker Hammer to manage the diazepam, for instance, doesn't quite bear thinking about—but it is a plan. Dr Garrett prints two copies, one each for Macca and Rowena to keep.

*

It is raining and the tram is full. The spines of somebody's wet umbrella needle her stockinged knees. Emily rubs the misted glass with her fist, makes a circle, peers through. Outside, people cling to the sides of buildings as they check out Tinder and Facebook on their smart phones. Above them, high on a red brick wall, graffiti hovers like a headline: *If you don't change direction soon, you may end up where you are heading.*

She thinks of Macca. She wonders if he is at home, taking the diazepam from Hammer, like he should be. She wonders where, exactly, home is. Is it a concrete unit covered in graffiti with aluminium foil in place of blinds? Or a crumbling shack with a yard full of beer bottles and thorny weeds?

As she daydreams, she tries to ignore Dr Jeff's mantra ringing in her ears: *Not your problem, not your problem, not your problem.*

He's late. Dr Garrett has called in the next patient, Kaylah, a teenager in her second trimester of pregnancy.

'So remember, there's still a small risk of listeria, so no soft cheeses or cold meats until after delivery.'

'Soft cheeses?'

'Feta, ricotta, brie...'

Kaylah screws up her face. 'Yuk.'

Dr Garrett helps the girl to her feet, guides her back to

the reception area. She is still typing in the teenager's notes when she hears a rhythmic tap on the door.

'Betcha thought I'd gone AWOL.'

'Macca.'

He is alive. And he looks sober.

'How are you?' she asks.

'Been better.'

He has bags beneath his eyes, but his hair is washed and he seems happy.

'The shakes?'

'Getting there.'

'Any diazepam today?'

'Five mils. At ten o'clock.'

'How's Hammer?'

'Reckon he's found his calling.'

Dr Garrett laughs. She opens Macca's file on the computer.

'Seeing Em on the weekend,' he says, his voice faltering. 'Missus says she's proud of me.'

The printer bursts to life, a shuddering monster of grey plastic between them. Dr Garrett hands him the prescription.

'Macca, that's wonderful.'

'Wouldn't be the first time,' Rowena says.

Dr Garrett wants to shake her—force some emotion into that vacuous face. Macca has vanished. Not even the good old Hammer knows where he is. He has slipped off into the night with a hipflask full of scotch and two pairs of Hammer's old jocks. It's not supposed to be this way, Dr Garrett thinks. He is supposed to be here—abstinent and smiling—thanking her and patting her on the back.

'He's in breach of his court order,' she says.

'Yes.'

'What will happen to him?'

Rowena shrugs. 'Police'll catch up with him, I guess.' She picks up her bag. 'It's been nice working with you,' she says, avoiding eye contact.

Dr Garrett tells herself that he won't pick up. A blocked number could be his wife, or the police, or—and perhaps worst of all—*her*. Because she is probably the last person he wants to hear from. A reminder of all his failings. Another name, another Emily, to add to the long list of women he has disappointed. But she is wrong. Just as she is about to hang up, he answers.

'Hello?'

He sounds relaxed, almost casual.

'Macca? It's Dr Garrett.'

She can hear him breathing. Deep exhalations, like he's smoking. 'G'day, doc.'

'How are you?'

'Okay.' He exhales again. 'On me way to Darwin.'

Dr Garrett wants to plunge her fingers into her ears, tell him not to tell her any more.

'Working holiday.'

She laughs. There is a muffled sound of men talking.

'I've gotta go.'

'Yes, of course. I just wanted to make sure…as you missed your appointment.'

'No worries.'

She hears the beep of a car horn.

'And doc?'

'Yes?'

'She'll be right.'

He hangs up. But it's too soon. Dr Garrett hasn't finished with him yet. She hasn't had time to make him understand that she is simply fulfilling her duty of care; that he is no more special to her than any of her other poor and homeless patients; that—in spite of the impression she may have given him—deep down, she doesn't care.

Clear Blue Seas

DAY 1

The seaplane settles on the water with the lightness of an insect. Propellers slow. The ocean, momentarily ruffled, is calm again. At the jetty an army of staff wait with frosted champagne glasses. Passengers alight and swap their bags for keys on wooden turtle key chains.

It had been Raf's idea to come to the Maldives. Kat would have preferred Cuba, or even Sri Lanka—somewhere a little less clichéd. For months they'd flipped through brochures of white beaches and couples with airbrushed skin and Kat suppressed horror at the prices in tiny type beneath the glossy prints. When she forgot herself and Raf mistook her disgust for some kind of disbelieving awe, he took her shoulders in his hands and told her, in a soft voice, that there was no such thing as his money or her money. Which was easy for him to say. He wasn't the one dropping small change from freelance writing jobs into the pool of his six-figure salary.

A Thai woman who introduces herself as Sukhon shows them to their room. They follow her down a sandy path flanked with coral-coloured bougainvillea. Hidden behind a hibiscus sits a mud hut with a neat straw roof. Sukhon opens the door and removes her slippers before beckoning them inside. She kneels between two footbaths with floating frangipani flowers at the end of the four-poster bed. She points to Kat's Havaiana thongs and Raf's leather moccasins.

'Oh no,' Kat says, looking at Raf. 'We couldn't possibly.'

'I am the head masseuse on the island,' Sukhon says and stands up. 'I specialise in reflexology.'

She shows them how to operate the air conditioning before shuffling backwards to the door. Somehow, during this brief deferential dance, Raf slips Sukhon a tip. Kat is both impressed and a little revolted. She has always felt uneasy about wads of money pressed deep into waiting palms.

DAY 2

Raf is asleep. He lies on his stomach, face buried in the pillow, brown arms flung carelessly across the bed. Kat watches the morning light snake across the valleys of his naked back. *Husband*. The word feels awkward and foreign on her newly married lips. She never dreamt of being part of this club—this world of Thermomixes and LCD TVs. She thinks back to her beaming smile at the ceremony and hates herself just a little.

It was five years ago now that Raf had burst into her world of lightless share houses and homemade bongs like a gust of cool clean air. She'd only ever dated boys who got stoned and pierced their eyebrows with safety pins. Raf's recollections of life in war-ravaged Iraq were horrifying, authentic. Better than her memories of paddle pools and Scrabble games, which played like some reel from *The Wonder Years* in the dusty corners of her mind. But he scared her too. His whole family did. Because the humble, gentle people who fussed over her at dinner and cried at the mere suggestion of grandchildren didn't match the steely characters from Raf's stories. Kat found it hard to picture Raf's mother— a woman who made little eye contact and cupped her hand to her mouth when she laughed—sheltering beneath a bed as bullets tore through her house, or Raf's milky-eyed father pulling a limbless man from a smouldering building on his way home from work. She often marvelled, too, at how a boy who wet the bed until he was ten and chewed his fingernails until they bled could one day become a celebrated barrister in Australia.

Raf wakes. Without opening his eyes, he grabs Kat's legs and pulls her onto his hips. They make love in the efficient but not unenjoyable way unique to married couples. When they are finished, Kat finds her underwear among the sheets and then pads, barefoot, to the ensuite.

The decor of the bathroom is in keeping with the resort's Robinson Crusoe theme. The tiles are a seamless constellation of pebbles—too smooth and regular to be natural—and the bath is a perfect oval cut into a block of dark grey stone. Kat brushes her teeth, rinses and wipes her mouth with a fluffy towel. When she opens her eyes, she sees Raf's sleep-crumpled face in the mirror.

'Nice touch,' Kat says, pointing to a sign above the sink.

> DEAR GUESTS, EVERY DAY MILLIONS OF GALLONS
> OF WATER ARE USED TO WASH TOWELS THAT HAVE
> ONLY BEEN USED ONCE. A TOWEL ON THE RACK
> MEANS 'I WILL USE AGAIN.'

'A towel on the floor means *I'm an arsehole*,' Raf says.

Kat laughs.

'Ironic, isn't it?' he adds.

She doesn't follow.

'A place soon to be drowned beneath the sea is pleading with us to save water.'

*

DAY 3

The waiter studies the horizon as he flicks a napkin across Kat's lap.

'Coffee?' he says, to nobody in particular.

Raf nods.

They are falling into a routine. They wake up at the same time and they sit at the same table on the beach with an unobstructed view of the ocean.

Raf pushes back his chair, ploughing deep troughs in the sand with its legs. While he gathers food, Kat reads the news—a one-page summary of the *New York Times* with too many typos to mention. Another lone wolf terrorist attack. Another high school massacre. Another photo of President Obama at another talkfest on climate change. She sips her coffee and folds the news into a crude paper aeroplane.

Raf returns with half the buffet balanced precariously on his plate.

'I got a bit carried away.'

Kat stands up. It's her turn. She wanders around the tables, lost amid the mountains of food. Watermelon carved into a lotus flower. Mangoes bursting out of their skins. Plain croissants, almond croissants, pains au chocolat, pains aux raisins. Blueberry friands, raspberry friands, apple friands. Blistered sausages and curled rashers of bacon and a hollandaise sauce like liquid gold. And at the centre of it all, a chef in a stiff white hat, making eggs and pancakes to order.

'Just one, please, sunny side up.'

The chef says nothing. Kat wonders if he has heard her, but then he ignites a ring on his stovetop. He looks at the pan, at the bowl of chopped chives in front of him, anywhere but her expectant face. She holds out her plate and he slides the egg onto it. The yolk quivers like something alive. She waits for it to stop.

'Thank you.'

The chef scrapes his spatula across the bottom of the pan. It makes an awful, nails-on-blackboard noise. He doesn't look up.

When Kat returns to the table, Raf's plate is clean and his face is deep in a diving book. He is going for his thirty-metre certification. Any excuse for an exam. Kat sits down, pokes violent holes in the yolk sac with her fork.

Raf looks up. 'You all right?'

She watches the amber fluid ooze across her plate. 'Not the friendliest of people, is he?'

'Who?'

'That chef.'

Raf looks over at the buffet. A woman in a hot-pink bikini has ordered a crepe. The chef flips it in a perfect arc above his clean white paper hat.

'What do you expect?' Raf says, dropping his sunglasses

over his eyes. 'It's Ramadan. Poor guy's probably starving.'

'Ramadan. Of course,' Kat says, feeling stupid. Ignorant and stupid.

DAY 4

As Raf descends into the ocean, Kat takes a tour of the capital, which is on another island, just nearby. It is not a popular destination. There are only four other people on the boat: a mother and daughter from New Zealand and a gay couple from San Francisco. There is no beach in sight. Only scooters and gold-capped mosques and bright square buildings that look like Lego. A tour guide greets them at the dock and helps the group disembark. He is a small man named Ali with dancing eyes and a porcelain smile.

'Ten years ago we were hit by the tsunami.'

They nod, frowning, remembering their Christmas bellies and a number of dead too obscene to be believed.

'Two-thirds of Malé was flooded. A hundred people died. The resort island you are staying on now disappeared.' He makes a flattening motion with his hands. 'Completely. Under. Water.'

Ali smiles as he talks, proud of his people's capacity for regeneration, but Kat feels disoriented. She remembers that day: post-break-up, drunk, passed out on her mum's leather recliner. And it couldn't have been ten years ago—she is not old enough to talk in decades.

They visit Malé's handful of attractions on foot: the Sultan Park, the National Museum, the Islamic Centre, the presidential palace. But talk of the tsunami stays with them. The gay couple had a friend who drowned on Koh Phi Phi. The New Zealand girl had flown out of Aceh a day before the monster wave hit.

On the way home, the hum of the boat's engine and the diesel fumes combine to have a tranquil effect. Kat stares at the water. She pictures Raf thirty metres down, kept alive by a cylinder of air on his back. The more she stares, the more she thinks she can see the insidious rise of the water's surface with each deep and heaving breath.

DAY 5

They're in the lounge, watching the rain fall in beaded curtains around them. Raf is checking his email.

'The dealership emailed me. The car will be ready next week.'

Kat nods. He's like a child, she thinks, with an eighty-thousand-dollar toy. She doesn't look up from her book.

'Metallic red. Ruby, they call it. With satellite navigation.'

He thinks these things will convince her: a sexy colour, a built-in mapping device. A waiter clears Raf's plate. He asks if there will be anything else.

'I could do with another coffee,' Raf says. 'But can I have it brought to the room?'

The waiter says, 'Yes, of course, sir,' before disappearing through the kitchen's double doors. Raf returns to his emails. Kat closes her book.

'Do you ever feel bad?'

Raf smiles. 'Can you be more specific?'

But she's not in a joking mood. 'Forget it.'

The smile vanishes. When he speaks again, his voice is tight. 'You can't say something like that and then tell me to forget it.'

She studies the ocean through the haze of rain. It is more a cloudy grey, now, than turquoise.

'You know,' Raf says, leaning across the table that sits between them like an island, 'any of these people would swap places with you in a heartbeat.'

'These people?'

'And they'd enjoy themselves.'

She searches for her page again in the book, pretends she's no longer listening.

'Not agonising over whether the coffee they're drinking is fair-trade.'

He is referring to another cafe. Another city. Another fight.

'You'd have had it, wouldn't you?' she snaps. 'If I hadn't stepped in.'

'Had what?'

'The footbath. You'd have let her give you one.'

He rolls his eyes. 'It's a footbath, Kat. Not a blow job.'

The bartender bends his head, polishes glasses intently.

'You didn't answer the question.'

Raf stands up, clamps his laptop beneath his arm.

'So shoot me.'

DAY 6

They carve out their spaces: she, in the rattan armchair, buried in a book; he propped up in bed, doing serious things on his computer. By midmorning, Kat can't bear it anymore. She leaves the hut to go for a walk. Today she ventures further than usual, to a low fence at the end of the beach. There is no gate, but she scales it easily enough in her thongs and running shorts. Beyond the fence, a bougainvillea grows wild and frantic in leafy violet clumps. She picks her way through the thorny branches. Green claws catch on her skin. Through the purple flowers, she sees a paved clearing and a grey slab of building that eclipses the sun.

A few shirtless men are playing a game of basketball in a fenced-off central courtyard. Kat recognises one of them as the breakfast chef. The men shout and laugh and slap each other's sweaty backs. Even though she is twenty metres away, Kat can smell the rows of salted fish drying in the concrete quadrangle, and the rubbish, piled high in plastic bags, outside the gate to the compound.

Someone pats Kat on the shoulder. She turns around with a start.

'You don't belong here,' Sukhon says, pulling her free from the thorny nest.

How long has she been there—hiding between the leaves, spying on Kat as she spies on the staff—before finally making her presence known?

She holds Kat's hand all the way back to the beach but says nothing until she turns to go.

'Your hut is over there.'

DAY 7

'Our last night on the island.'

It is dusk, and Kat and Raf are making their way to farewell drinks at the restaurant.

'We should've been more aggressive at Tribal Council.'

Kat laughs. She remembers drinking cheap beer and watching *Survivor* on his parents' leather lounge suite.

'You look nice,' he says.

She is wearing the apricot-coloured dress she wore the night he proposed. She chose it especially.

'Thanks.'

Cicadas hum. The sun casts pink and purple shadows at their feet. As they round the bend, they see four men sitting cross-legged on the sand with drums between their knees.

'Bodu beru,' Raf says. 'Made from stingray hide.'

This is what Kat loves most about him. His worldliness. One of the men knocks two bamboo sticks together. The other three close their eyes. They tap a beat on the drums. Gently sway.

Sukhon is holding a tray of champagne flutes. Kat and Raf take one each. The chef stands behind a platter of seafood. Sashimi slices arranged in a fan. Ice glinting like diamonds. Lemons like polished gems.

Couples mill about the tables, the women in loose summer dresses, the men in candy-coloured shorts. On each table lies a placard with the lyrics of a Maldivian folk song.

> *On the horizon of the vast Indian Ocean grow green palms*
> *This is my homeland, this is the Maldives*
> *From the clear blue seas, we grow like pearls*
> *This is my homeland, this is the Maldives*

Raf pulls Kat away from the party, out of reach of the candlelight. He kisses her, in the darkness, with a warm, open mouth. The air is still. There are no clouds. Stars— long dead—wink at some shared celestial joke. And all the while, the ocean wraps its black arms around the island. Sleeping. Breathing. Waiting.

Ticket-holder Number 5

For as long as she could remember, Tania had carried a canister of capsicum spray in her workbag. She'd never had cause to use it, but she believed it was only a matter of time. Last Christmas Eve, Sheila from the Dandenong office had been verbally abused by a customer—some derro who said her mouth looked like a cat's arse and that he wanted to slash her from ear to ear. Poor thing had to take three whole months off work. And when she did come back—at significantly reduced hours, mind you—she'd only managed one shift before breaking down and begging her manager for a transfer.

Anna from customer service said that even now, almost a year down the track, Sheila couldn't sleep unless she drank a whisky or took a sleeping pill. Post-traumatic stress, they called it, like what soldiers get after the war. Which made a lot of sense to Tania. Because sometimes that's what it felt like. War. Tania versus the guy done for drunk driving who came in early for his licence. Tania versus the taxi driver from Pakistan who slipped her a fifty in the sleeve of his road rules book. Tania versus the pensioner with cloudy corneas who recited the eye chart from memory. They made her sick. She tried to hide it behind smiling eyes and a gentle I-give-a-shit voice, but she knew that one day, when she wasn't on top of her game—when she had come down with a cold or hadn't had enough sleep or was late getting out to lunch—one of the smarter ones would see her distaste like a crack across her broken face and they would snap like the derro had with Sheila that day in the Dandenong office, and that's when she would be waiting, like a cowboy in the movies, with her hand on the cold metal canister of capsicum spray.

Tania parked her Daihatsu and swiped herself through the back door. Thank God for the back door. Once upon a time she'd had to plough through the mob at the front entrance, all bitching and smoking as they counted down the minutes to nine am.

Counter 3. Her office: an eighty-centimetre square of bench-space between two thick perspex plates. They were not supposed to have personal items cluttering the area—random spot inspections occurred approximately twice a year—but Tania had made it her own with a photo of her two-year-old granddaughter and a picture of a beach she'd ripped out of a *Women's Weekly*.

Ticket-holder number 5 drove a 2008 Honda sedan. She had the frightened look of someone surviving on shots of espresso and adrenaline.

'How can I help you today?' Tania asked with a smile.

'My husband's dead.' Her voice was flat and lifeless, as if it had died along with her husband.

Tania pulled out the box of tissues she kept for such occasions in the top drawer of her desk.

'The car was in his name.' For what seemed like a long time, the widow sat and stared at an invisible spot behind Tania's head.

'And you'd like the vehicle's registration transferred into your name,' Tania suggested after several minutes had passed.

'Yes.'

Tania licked her index finger and retrieved the relevant form—easily recognisable by its lime-green colour—from the organiser on her desk. 'You'll need to fill this out and bring it back, together with your husband's original death certificate.' She cleared her throat. 'Plus the transfer fee.'

The woman took the form in her bony, blue-veined

hands. She frowned, as if contemplating what to do with it: eat it, preserve it or, in an angry rage, destroy it.

Tania looked at her watch. It was nine-twenty-three. The queue was making its frustration known with dramatic sighs and restless shifting feet. She would have to move this widow along, and quickly.

She had just composed her concluding remark—a perfect amalgamation of sensitivity and no-nonsense expediency—when she heard it. A loud plopping sound, like the first fat drops of rain. But it was not rain. It was tears. The widow's tears, exploding on the green canopy of paper.

'I have copies of his death certificate,' she said, placing two crumpled documents on the desk. 'But the person I spoke to on the phone didn't say I'd need the original too.'

Tania shifted the tissue box a little closer to the woman's hand.

'I have a three-year-old at home. Brie. And I'm thirteen weeks pregnant.' The woman touched a spot below her navel. 'We just bought a house and we have two hundred thousand dollars of debt and even though I know he's dead, I can't stop saying *we*.'

Tania held out a tissue. With her eyes she implored the woman to wipe her melting face.

'I need to sell the car. But I can't do it unless it's in my name.'

People had cried in front of Tania before, many times—

on average once per week—but she had never given in to them, no matter how sad the story. On the odd occasion that she had felt herself softening as she listened to their sorry tale, she reminded herself of her own struggle: her father's handprint, a bloodied stamp, across her mother's sunken face; raising Leah from the age of two as a single mum; waking up after having her breast and its walnut-sized cancer removed at the premature age of thirty-one. Nobody had cut her any slack and she had managed to survive. She was probably even better for it. Hardened. Inured. Unbreakable, almost.

But today was different. There was something about this widow and her spiky words that struck at Tania's heart like a mace. The overall effect was one of disorientation: of being bombarded with so many emotions at once that it was impossible to focus on just one. All she wanted to do was get away, get to some place where she could breathe again. And in her desperation to escape, she broke a cardinal rule of customer service. She said: 'I'll see what I can do.'

The tearoom was empty. Relieved, Tania steadied herself at the sink. Her boss spent Sunday nights screwing Anna from customer service and Monday mornings sleeping in. He didn't answer his phone before ten am, and even if he did, Tania wasn't going to call him. She wasn't going to beg him for a concession she knew he would never make, a concession that she—hard-arse Tania as he liked to call her, before giving her a good slap on the bum—would never request.

She called Leah instead.

'I told you not to call me at work,' her daughter said.

'Sorry.'

'Is it an emergency?'

'No. It was a mistake.'

'What was a mistake?'

'Calling you.'

'Are you sure everything's okay?'

'I dunno, Leah, you're the psych nurse. You tell me.'

'Mum…'

'Nothing's wrong. Just checking in, making sure that little Bella's okay.'

'She's fine.'

'And Eric?'

'Since when did you give a shit about Eric?'

'Never mind.'

'Now you really have got me worried.' There was a scream followed by a loud bang. 'Look, Mum, I've gotta go, but I'll come round when I finish work. I'll bring leftovers. We'll have coffee, watch *Farmer Wants a Wife*.'

When Tania returned, the woman had wiped the mascara from her cheeks and was sitting straight-backed in the chair.

'I can go home and get the original.'

'That won't be necessary,' Tania said, surprised at the

pleasure she gleaned from the disbelief on the widow's face. 'I've sighted the original, and I'm satisfied.'

'But—'

Tania held up her hand. She stamped the documents. 'You'll receive the rest of the papers in the post. They should be there by the end of the week.'

An ever so faint pink, like the colour of cherry blossoms, flushed the widow's pale cheeks.

'Thank you.'

But Tania couldn't bear to look at her.

'Thank you,' the woman said again.

Kevin, from the adjacent cubicle, leaned back in his chair and pointed to his Casio watch. He was fastidious about his appearance, from his bushranger hair and thick-framed glasses all the way down to his Astro Boy socks.

'I was starting to worry that Tania the Great had taken a fall from her golden perch.' He had not yet forgiven her for spilling punch on his limited edition Reebok sneakers at last year's Christmas party.

'It's all under control, Kevin.'

'And then I saw who you were dealing with.'

'I have work to do, Kevin.'

'I forget the name. Alice, or Alicia, or something equally pedestrian.'

Alice Pickering.

'She was in here last week. Some sob-story about her brother dying in a car crash and needing the rego transferred into her name.' Kevin laughed. 'No documents. Nothing. Just unwashed hair and one hell of a performance.'

Tania gripped the edge of the desk. She watched the slow bleach of her knuckles.

'She should've gone into acting. Better than Cate Blanchett or Nicole Kidman. Almost had me fooled. She was really...' Kevin chewed on his lip as he searched for the perfect word. 'Authentic.'

In the queue, a teenager with a scorpion tattoo was cursing his girlfriend on the phone. A frazzled mother looked poised to smack a toddler, who was pounding sultanas into the floor. A pensioner's malfunctioning hearing aid stabbed the air with its high-pitched ring.

Tania pressed the big red button that directed the next ticket-holder to her desk. As she waited, she forced herself to think of Sheila and the derro in the Dandenong office. She willed herself to remember the man's needless violence and Sheila's long and sleepless nights. She imagined that it had been Leah, or a grown-up Bella, whose face the derro had threatened to slash from ear to ear. And then, choked with indignation, she plunged her hand inside her workbag and felt for the cold metal canister of capsicum spray.

Hotel Cambodia

Through the brown shields of her sunglasses, she watches her flesh sweat like a Sunday roast. Beside her, ice cubes pop and crackle in a glass of Diet Coke. Soon she will slip into the pool. But not yet. For now the heat is bearable. She will wait for the prickle and the pain.

A volunteer at the NGO had warned her about the end of the dry season. Melissa had looked at his Celtic skin—papery stuff destined to sprout skin cancers like tiny horns in old age—and inwardly scoffed. Unlike him, she had Asian heritage. Her colouring was a direct result of ancestors toiling, knee deep, in rice paddies under the sun. Never mind that she had grown up in air-conditioned apartments in Singapore, or that her own mother was of Anglo-Celtic background. In this instance, she would abide by the old Australian adage: *She'll be right*.

But she wasn't right. During her first twenty-four hours in Phnom Penh, she didn't pee, not even a drop, her kidneys trapping fluid like some super-strength sponge. And as she consumed litre after litre of 'mineral' water—which she suspected was rebottled tap water—she observed locals on motodops in flannelette pyjamas and skinny jeans with nothing short of pure awe.

Now, after three months of sweat and thirst, she can don jeans with the best of them. On bad days, of which there are many, she wonders if this is her greatest accomplishment. But then she scolds herself for her cynicism. Nobody forced this upon her. Nobody was in the room cheering her on when she googled the words *NGO* and *Cambodia* and *nurse*. And though many colleagues applauded her altruism, another friend had said, 'What's with you white people going to third world countries and making yourselves *uncomfortable*?' At which point she had blushed and said nothing, because, while strictly speaking she was not white, she had lived a privileged existence compared to him.

Melissa takes off her sunglasses and stands up. In the shallows, a Khmer girl of about fifteen frolics with a younger boy. Aside from a bored waiter, they are the only three people at the pool. She dives in. The cool water is like a balm against her sunburnt skin. There is a froth of bubbles, brown legs, muffled shrieks. She lets her body float, arms stretched in surrender to the blistering sun. It is here and only here that she can come close to forgetting: a motorcyclist's skull, cracked open like a coconut, blood forming a black ribbon in the dust; a tearless woman holding her cleft-lipped baby to the van's windscreen, for sale, like a sack of rice; row after row of ramshackle brothels full of teenagers in Tweety Bird pyjamas. Here, for a measly five US dollars, she can pretend she is just another tourist, relaxing after a week of marvelling at the detailed carvings at Angkor Wat.

She swims to the edge of the pool, rests her elbows on the tiles. A man with a hairy gut emerges from the change room. She can tell immediately from his board shorts and thongs that he is Australian. He heaves himself onto a lounge, wheezes in and out.

Melissa has met many expats since arriving in Phnom Penh. There was the Christian missionary who had returned from a day in the provinces, flushed and smug, after 'saving' one of the minority Cham people from the clutches of Islam. There was the vegan aid worker who—in a managerial position he would never have landed back home—prided himself on the number of Khmer friends he could call his own. And then there was the British pensioner in the foot massage parlour who moaned, as if in the throes of orgasm, while a teenager yanked on his toes. Melissa would like to think she is better than all of them, but sometimes she's not so sure. After all, she had only looked to Cambodia when the hospitals in Melbourne failed to provide the validation she'd been searching for. At the idealistic age of eighteen, she had chosen a career in health to make a difference, save lives, change the world, and Cambodia, with its reputation for tragedy, seemed like just the place to do it.

Brian had picked her up from the airport. He and his wife were devout Christians who had left their grown sons in Arkansas to establish a women's refuge south of Phnom Penh. Brian was tall with dreadlocks and a wardrobe of paisley shirts. He looked like an extra from *Jesus Christ Superstar*. In the car, he told Melissa how he'd found God late in life after what he hinted was a less than pure past. God had given him sobriety and clarity and an opinion, it seemed, on everything. What affection Melissa lacked for Brian, she reserved for his wife, Hope, a retired short-order cook with a gentle voice and a huge heart.

And so it was that Melissa moved in with the loving evangelical couple from the States, who treated her like a prodigal daughter. Every morning, before a breakfast of bacon and eggs, she held hands with Brian and Hope under the table as Brian said a lengthy grace. Breakfast was followed by a cold shower—something Melissa had found difficult at first, but which she now asserted was a refreshing start to the day—and then she dressed in her uniform of long skirt and modest long-sleeved top. When she was ready, she stepped through the gates of the compound to a chorus of motodop drivers yelling 'Lady!' and finally haggled a good price for one of them to take her the short distance to Antoine's clinic.

Antoine, like many foreigners in Cambodia, was something of a maverick. He'd been born in Montreal, but for decades he had called the small apartment above the clinic in Phnom Penh home. Though he loved to smoke and drink and joke around, nobody really knew much about him. Some claimed he had started out as a cardiologist in Canada but fled after a procedure on a patient had gone horribly wrong. Others speculated he had French-Cambodian heritage and was simply returning home. A Khmer doctor once told Melissa he had spied a crumpled photo of a Cambodian girl—a daughter or lover, perhaps?—in Antoine's wallet. But the mystery surrounding Antoine only made the expat community love him more. The patients were eternally grateful to him, always keen to share a story about how the Canadian doctor had saved their life, or their arse. Certainly it was a change from Australia. Antoine lorded it over everyone from his perch on the front step of the clinic, cigarette in hand. Between consultations, the other doctors conferred about their crudely constructed management plans. They set fractures on drunks with little, if any, anaesthetic. They watched a Khmer nurse jump on a distressed-but-very-much-alive patient's chest and, for reasons unclear to all of them, commence cardiac compressions. It was shocking and terrifying and exhilarating. But the skills Melissa learnt in a private practice devoted to expatriates—how to treat dengue fever with intravenous fluids and dispense chlamydia treatments like lollies—did nothing to prepare her for the malnutrition and post-traumatic stress she would encounter in the provinces. The young father with leukaemia who couldn't afford a blood transfusion. The mother of three with HIV banished to a hut on the edge of the village. For the most part, the expats got better. The Khmer, dehydrated and overworked and terrorised by their past, almost never did.

But it was bearable, because every Sunday, while Brian and Hope went to church, she could come here, to Hotel Cambodia. Within its high brick walls, she could get her weekly fix of luxury, and tranquillity, and reality. Or unreality. Because she couldn't tell anymore.

Melissa goes for one last swim. She feels the water smooth her hair, dissolve the grime from her face. In the shallows, where the Khmer kids are playing, two feet hang like slabs of dough beneath the surface. When she looks up, she sees that they belong to the Australian man. He sits on the edge of the pool—a hirsute freckled hulk—as the children orbit like satellites around him. When she'd first arrived, she might have tried to tell herself that the Khmer kids were the Australian man's adopted grandchildren, that he headed an orphanage and was taking two lucky orphans for a swimming lesson. But she has driven past the cardboard brothels late at night. She has seen seven-year-olds wearing rouge and lipstick and high heels. She knows there is an area in the red-light district nicknamed 'Kiddies Corner'. Her brain spews out images like some rogue polaroid camera. Blackout curtains. Carpet stains. Mini bottles of brandy.

As she dries herself with a towel, she keeps one eye on the threesome. The children laugh and play and splash in the water while the man leans back on his hands, his belly thrust before him. They could run, she thinks. It would be easy enough for them to get away from him. He is too fat, too wheezy to catch them, no matter how malnourished they may be. But there are invisible strings. She sees that now. The boy and girl are little more than marionettes, tied to the promise of a better life—at the very least, a hot meal.

One day Brian had taken her to the rubbish dump. She had heard tales about the people who lived on top of the steaming mound, but to actually behold it was a shock. The air that rose from the knoll of garbage was hot and pungent in ways she could never have imagined, and she followed Brian's lead and wrapped a kroma—the traditional Khmer scarf used as a sarong, towel, hat, blanket, sling—around her nose and mouth. They were with a Cambodian doctor who ran a mobile clinic at the dump once a month. Children gathered, grateful for the distraction from the boring task of collecting aluminium cans. A girl of twelve had infected scabies bites all over her bony shins. The doctor gave her a tube of cream and ten antibiotic tablets. He didn't move from his seat behind the folding table. He barely looked the child in the eye. A French woman from the NGO that sponsored the doctor snapped photographs for their summer newsletter.

That night, Melissa filled Hope with stories about her visit. But as she described her despair, Melissa heard something disturbing in her own voice—a childlike fascination or delight that came dangerously close to excitement. As if she were practising the tales she would tell her friends at the pub once she got back home to Australia.

The fat man is in the water now. Puffed and bloated, he looks less like a monster and more like a dying elephant seal. The children duck between his legs, dolphin-like, their skin brown and smooth and slick. She looks around. Apart from the waiter, there is nobody else to bear witness. But to what exactly? Even if there were a security guard who spoke English, she has nothing concrete to report. Only this gnawing feeling that sits like a rat beneath the curved blade of her breastbone.

The Australian man towels off. The girl helps him dry his back. The boy threads the thongs back onto his swollen feet. They pad across the blue tiles. Wet prints vanish in the heat. Melissa leans back, her mind awash with memories. Antoine, directing the clinic through a haze of typhoid fever, intravenous drip swinging from his arm. A tearful Hope, announcing, as if it were a revelation, that Khmer people grieve for their children too. The simultaneously pitying and satisfied look on Brian's face as he reads the Bible to a room full of farmers.

The sun is burning a hole through the teal arc of sky above her head. She feels it sting her legs, bite her crimson cheeks. The pool shimmers and beckons, but she will not return to its silent depths. Not today. Today she will sit with the pain.

Things That Grow

'This here's your problem,' he says, holding a tree root in his hands. 'If there's a leak, you can count on these thirsty buggers to find it.'

The plumber, whose name is Rob or Craig, promises me a quote by the end of the week. He gives me his card and says it's a big job, by way of a pre-emptive apology. I'm not surprised. When Paul and I moved in, there were mushrooms growing in the bathroom—shy things sprouting from the grout with bone-coloured bonnets. I remember joking about frying them up to eat with our steak and chips for dinner, but Paul said they were poisonous and threw them in the bin.

I look at the plumber's card. Turns out he is a Craig. I add it to the in-tray on Paul's sprawling mahogany desk.

The mail haunts me: every day there is another utility bill, another catalogue, another newsletter in his name. It's not clean, our cleavage from this world. We leave bits of ourselves behind: a hair fossilised in a bar of soap, a toenail clipping in the sink, our smell imbued in the fabric of our clothes and towels and pillows.

When the plumber leaves around ten am, I go to bed. I catch snippets of sleep. Mostly I stare at a patch of mildew on the ceiling that looks like the face of Jesus Christ. The night before the accident, Paul suggested we send a photo to *A Current Affair*. Or *Today Tonight*. We argued about which one. We spent two hours, some of the last we would ever spend together, debating the credibility of tabloid TV.

My phone vibrates across the floorboards. Mum. Now that Paul has gone, she's the only person—apart from my lawyer—who calls me.

'Cora.' She always sounds a little surprised when I answer, like she half-expected me to have topped myself in the night. 'How did you sleep?'

'With a valium.'

'You can't take those things forever.'

'It's been four weeks,' I say, rummaging for the bottle of tablets on the bedside table. 'That's hardly forever.'

She makes a noise that means: *I'm going to drop this now, but I know better.* 'Have you showered?' she asks.

'Can't.' I pop a tablet in my mouth and swallow it, dry,

just to spite her. 'Plumber says tree roots have invaded the bathroom.'

She sighs. I imagine her rolling her eyes. 'Why can't you just talk like a normal person?'

'I'm serious,' I say. 'Plants burrowing up through the grout, like a cancer.'

'Well, I told you not to buy from an owner-builder.' There it is again, that disappointment mixed with pleasure. Disappointment because I'm a failure, pleasure because it's all so beautifully in keeping with her carefully constructed world view. 'They never do the job properly. Aesthetics over quality.'

'God forbid.' My mother could never be accused of putting aesthetics over anything. 'Were you calling for a particular reason?' I ask.

'I'm dropping off some dinner later. A chicken curry. Around four-thirty.'

I don't need more food. The freezer is full of it. The only thing I can stomach is the odd cup of tea and, maybe, a Scotch Finger. But it's no use arguing with her.

'And for Chrissake, have a shower.'

Paul would be horrified by all this lazing around. He didn't tolerate idleness, or tardiness. We almost split up once on account of a broken-down train. It was pathological. I blamed his mother. He blamed his Swiss heritage.

Perhaps that's why—even from within my cocoon of grief—I feel guilty. Certainly there's some relief in allowing one day to bleed into the next, in not conforming to the social norms of breakfast, lunch and dinner, in guessing the hour from the way spears of light shoot through the venetian blinds. But ever since my nan passed away when I was sixteen, I've had the suspicion that the dead are watching our every move, that they see us standing naked before the bathroom mirror, plucking our hair and squeezing our pimples.

Around midday I pass out and have my first dream since the accident. Paul is there. I know it is him, even though he has the face of the plumber. He is wearing the wounds the emergency doctor checked off like a shopping list on his fingers: the depressed skull fracture; the flail chest; the pelvis shattered into bony shrapnel. But he is smiling. We are in a field of mushrooms and he is gliding towards me. I wake up before we touch, but not before I see the sky—clear but for a patch of cloud in the shape of Jesus Christ.

His mother insisted on burying him. She and I shared a chaise longue at the funeral parlour and flicked through wood swatches to an instrumental version of 'Wind Beneath My Wings'. We settled on the Amity Rose, a walnut-coloured casket with a sapphire blue lining. Paul would like it, his mother said, as if she had a direct line to his spirit, and the parlour director—a large man with leathery skin and a gruff laugh—agreed. 'Excellent choice,' he said. 'Very durable.'

After my nap I force myself to get dressed. It is the first day of spring and I sit on the small patch of grass in the backyard. The weather bureau has predicted an electrical storm, but for now the air is still. I can smell jasmine and fallen lemons and hear the distant chug of a lawnmower. Paul had terrible hay fever. On a day like today he would be holed up in the bedroom with the windows closed and the air conditioner on full blast. Nobody talked about that at the funeral, but these are the things I remember.

I close my eyes. The sun warms my cheeks. The weeds form a green wall around me. Beyond the fence I hear a sudden rustle of leaves. Must be that mongrel from next door.

Mary, Mary, quite contrary, how does your garden grow?

Or a child.

With silver bells and cockle shells and pretty maids all in a row.

I don't know my neighbours. Their bougainvillea has made a home of our fence, but we've barely exchanged a hello. I have vague memories of a woman with bushy eyebrows and two young kids—twins? I remember the dog better than the people: a yappy thing with the body of a Scottish terrier and a cheeky Jack Russell smile.

I peer through a gap in the fence. A girl is sitting on a blanket beneath a small jacaranda tree. A doll with matted hair and cloudy eyeballs is propped up against the trunk. The girl, who looks about three, pours the doll a cup of imaginary tea.

Mary, Mary, quite contrary, how does your garden grow?

It feels dirty to be hiding like this, watching a child, but I can't bring myself to look away. Something about the doll and the purple flowers feels familiar, like deja vu, or a dream.

With silver bells and cockle shells and pretty maids all in a row.

She stops. Suddenly she is looking straight at me with her big brown eyes, mouth open, on the verge of a scream.

My period is late. Yesterday, a doctor friend told me this was a physical manifestation of my grief—something about stress upsetting the hypothalamus. He suggested doing a pregnancy test. 'What's the harm in checking?' he said. I laughed, thinking he was joking, but his eyes were cold and serious.

This afternoon I buy a home pregnancy test from the chemist. When I drive home, Beethoven's fifth symphony is playing on the radio. My heart pounds along with the cymbals. If Paul were here, he would laugh at my melodrama. In the bathroom, I sit on the toilet, hold the wand between my legs and shower it with urine. Two minutes: the time it takes to make a cup of instant noodles or brush my teeth or freefall from an aeroplane. But I needn't wait. The two lines appear straight away. Pink and undeniable.

When Mum arrives at four-thirty, I run and hide in the master bedroom. I'm a teenager again, curled up in a ball with a blanket pulled over my head. She doesn't have a key—I won that argument—so she jumps the back fence. But I've thought of that too: the laundry blind is drawn and there is a chain on the back door.

'Cora? I know you're in there!' she shouts, but she doesn't sound too convinced.

She calls my phone five times and sends me three texts before finally leaving. It isn't malicious, this hibernation—it's a rite of passage. I need to feel the slow stretch of time, the unfurling of new limbs, the creaking of ancient roots.

Death blinds us. Now, when I see Paul, it's through a soft lens—the jerky product of a handheld camera, set to melancholic music. It seems almost blasphemous to recall the fight we had at Federation Square, the way pedestrians gave us a wide berth, the way they stared. Not to mention that adulterous text message I found but never mentioned, the awful banality of those blue, speech-bubbled words.

I wonder what Paul would say if he was here, if he knew. Almost certainly there would be touching: his hand on my neck, my arm, my stomach. He would half-joke about the baby playing footy, like him and his father before him. Because that was Paul—always leaping into the future, projecting ahead to his son in a footy jersey. And now, thinking these things as I lie curled in a pocket of air beneath my doona, it's not relief I feel at his absence, but it's not longing either. I throw back the covers and stare at Jesus on the ceiling, his eyes looking straight at me, at everything, at nothing.

The thing is, it's not the first time. I've been here before with Paul, in a different millennium. I know how the early part feels: the insatiable hunger, the paralysing fatigue, the breast tenderness, the pimples. Once it was done, we never spoke of it again. We were good at that—burying things. But it got harder when our friends started having babies: harder for me to suppress my sorrow, harder for Paul to ignore it.

On Friday, Craig the plumber calls.

'Did you get my quote?'

I had. It was outrageous.

'I'm still reeling,' I say and laugh. Craig the plumber doesn't. In his silence, I hear cartoons and a hysterical child yelling for daddy.

'You got kids?' he asks.

'No.'

'Lucky.' I hear him broker a deal involving an iPad and chocolate ice-cream. 'Well, if you do decide to go ahead, I can do next Monday or Tuesday.'

I look at the empty blister packs and the furry mouths of the mugs on my bedside table. 'I'll have to check with my husband.'

I listen to him negotiate with his children. Twenty minutes on the laptop. A double scoop with sprinkles.

'No worries,' he says before hanging up.

I go to bed to dream of him, in Robin Hood gear, hacking his way through a forest to save me.

For the first time in days, I take a shower. Standing beneath the water, I imagine tree roots exploding through the tiles and wrapping around my ankles. I think of my friend from high school who, after having her first baby, gave me a print of her placenta. I remember how Paul scrunched up his face and refused to touch it, as if it was contaminated, as if he could catch something. And I remember feeling queasy at the thought of the sac—still wet from the birth canal—being plopped like meat onto butcher's paper. But I also remember that I couldn't stop looking at it: the way the plaited cord wound its vine-like way up the white of the paper, the way the vessels splayed out to a billowing canopy of red.

There are no clean towels in the bathroom, and I stand wet and naked before the mirror. My body is keeping its secret behind a flat belly and pink nipples. I trace a line with my finger across the fleshy spot above my pubic bone.

Mary, Mary, quite contrary, how does your garden grow?

Water pools at my feet, staining the grey tiles black. A mushroom peeks through the grout. As I wrap myself in a robe that still smells vaguely of Paul, I marvel at this tiny being in the middle of my bathroom floor—so fragile I could lop its head off with a nudge of my big toe, and at the same time so stubborn, so insistent. I walk to the bedroom window and tug on the cord for the venetian blinds. With a snap like breaking bone, the room is bathed in light.

Fracture

The poster was Tony's grandson's idea. The family had gathered for their weekly Sunday meal. As usual, Carla had cooked up a storm. Roast pork, roast chicken, three salads and two cakes. They were all nursing their bellies, the adults drinking moscato and licking the last of the cheesecake from their plates, the kids lounging on beanbags as they watched a movie in the second living room.

Carla had been to mass in the morning, but Tony hadn't joined her. Tony hadn't seen the inside of a church since his wedding, forty years ago. He had given up on God when his father dropped dead from a heart attack the day he and Carla got back from their honeymoon. For Tony, it was the Sunday dinner that was the highlight of his week. To be flanked by family, and to have the old house resonating with noise, made Tony feel if not invincible then at least less vulnerable. Everybody listened as he told the story of the surgeon at the hospital. The family was outraged—Mario, his eldest son, the most so.

'You tell me his name. I'll make sure he gets what's coming to him.' Mario banged his fist on the table. The family knew it was an empty threat. In spite of his size—which, in recent years, was more fat than muscle—Mario was soft at heart. It was his late wife, Trudy, who had worn the pants in their little family, from the moment she gave birth to Luca in the back seat of a taxi to the moment she'd hit the ground in a tragic skydiving accident. The Ferraris missed her terribly. Now when they needed strength they looked to her ferocious son.

Luca said nothing as he listened to his nonno's story. When Tony had finished and the others had taken turns to voice their disbelief, Luca slunk away. About an hour later, when Carla had just started clearing everyone's plates, he returned, wielding a piece of paper.

'Is this the guy?' he said, holding up the poster proudly, like a five-year-old. The family stopped talking. They looked at the grainy head shot and read the caption in huge capitals below it.

* * *

Below his face was one word: *FUCKWIT.* It was Anzac Day, and Deepak wondered if the timing was deliberate—the naming and shaming of an antihero, or something along those lines—but he didn't think the perpetrator was capable of such sophistication. The poster was amateurish. His photo had been downloaded from the hospital website and then blown up to ten times its size. Fortunately he'd gone to work early that day—the registrar had called at seven am about a girl who had fractured her arm. When Deepak saw the poster near the main entrance, he immediately tore it down, but he felt dirty—as if he had something to hide—when he buried it in an infectious waste bin.

Public holidays were always busy and Anzac Day was no different. A fractured femur, a supracondylar, two dislocated shoulders, in addition to the usual rubbish from the ward. By ten o'clock that night, as Deepak collapsed into Simone's bed, the poster was a million miles from his mind. He only thought of it the next morning when he woke up, naked and sticky from sex.

'Do you know who it was?' Simone asked when he told her the story.

He shook his head.

'But do you have your suspicions?'

Deepak thought of the hundreds of patients he'd operated on over the years. Some were disgruntled, of course—you could never please everyone—but nobody stood out to him.

'Fuck,' Simone said, twisting her blond hair into a knot on top of her head. 'I'd have a short list of twenty.' She stood up and walked to the bathroom. Through the hiss of the shower, she shouted an inventory of all the patients who'd made complaints about her over the years. But it was little comfort to Deepak. Simone was one of the top orthopaedic surgeons in Australia. Last year she'd won a prestigious women's leadership award. Simone could easily rebuff such an attack. Deepak, on the other hand, was a junior consultant. He had failed his oral exams three times—when he was stressed he had a stutter.

Deepak picked a strand of Simone's hair off the pillow and draped it over his palm. He'd never been with a blond before. Growing up, he'd joked about it with his friends at high school—other brown-skinned boys who confused screwing a blond with screwing white imperialism—but they were fourteen at the time and none of them had done anything with a girl other than pashing. He wound the hair around his finger, watched his fingertip swell with blood. Here was the *hair spun of gold* he had read about, as a child, in fairytales. If he said this to Simone, she would baulk at his sentimentality, tell him it was all ammonia-based chemicals. Even so, Deepak couldn't quite believe he shared his bed with this woman. She had grown up in the eastern suburbs of Melbourne, spending holidays surfing at Anglesea or snowboarding at Mount Hotham. Deepak had spent summers with his best friend, Prakash, stealing porn magazines from the local milk bar.

Simone emerged from the shower, pink and smooth and sleek. She towelled off in front of him. 'Don't worry about the poster,' she said.

'I'm not.'

'Just some nut case.' Her perfect breasts jiggled and bounced. 'It'll blow over.'

Once she left, Deepak got dressed. He'd promised his parents he would visit them. The air outside was crisp, and he put on the beanie and scarf he kept in his car. He left Simone's warehouse apartment in Fitzroy and drove to his parents' house in Sunshine. Deepak's mother loved telling her family in London she lived in a place called Sunshine. Never mind that it was an old industrial district, or that the nearest beach was fifteen kilometres away. In twenty years her English relatives had never paid a visit.

Deepak's father was out the front of the house, pruning the roses. He covered his ears with his hands as his son parked in the driveway. 'I could hear your car all the way from the Ring Road,' he said when Deepak got out of the Porsche.

'That's what I paid a year's salary for.'

His father shook his head and turned back to his rosebushes.

'Where's Mum?'

'Cooking.'

Deepak went inside. He let the smell of roasting spices and the 'meadows and rain' air freshener his mother had been buying for years waft over him. His mum was standing at the kitchen bench reading *New Idea* before a backdrop of bubbling pots and pans.

'Smells good.'

'Did you know that Norah Jones is half-Indian?' his mother said, putting down the magazine and turning her attention back to the stove. 'She was born Geetali Norah Shankar.'

Deepak laughed. 'I'd change my name too if I was called Shankar.' He lifted the lid of one of the pans. His mum slapped his hand.

'Shankar is a very common Indian name.'

'Yeah, I know. But it sounds the same as *chancre*, which is a genital sore caused by syphilis.'

His mother shook her head. 'When did you get so dirty?'

Deepak opened the fridge. He took out the orange juice and drank it straight from the carton.

'They divorced, of course.'

'Who?'

'Norah Jones' parents.'

Deepak threw the empty juice carton into the box his mother used for recycling. 'Who the hell is Norah Jones?'

'A singer.' She turned away from her cauldrons and looked at Deepak. 'Mixed marriages never work. Too many cultural barriers.'

His parents didn't know about Simone. Once, his mother had asked him about the pretty blond on his Facebook page, but she seemed satisfied when Deepak said she was a work colleague.

Secrecy was convenient for Simone, too. *People will talk*, she said if Deepak grabbed her bottom when no one was looking. *I'm your boss*. But Deepak wondered if it wasn't more than that. Simone's father was a member of the Melbourne Club and the owner of a racehorse called Pink Diamond. When Simone showed Deepak pictures of her family and friends at the Melbourne Cup, he couldn't spot a brown face among them.

For years Deepak's parents had been setting him up on blind dates with successful Indian women. Deepak played along, because sometimes it was quite fun and deep down he really did want to please them. Lately, though—presumably because of the advancing age of the women he was being set up with—the meetings felt less like bonding sessions about crazy Indian parents and more like interrogation. Nowadays the women had sharp nails and pursed lips. They knew what they wanted in a man, and they were determined to find out, over a three-hour degustation, if Deepak had it.

Simone was fascinated by these introductions and spent hours grilling him about the details. While Deepak knew he should be grateful to have such an open-minded girlfriend, in truth, he was disappointed. Just once, as he described an encounter with one of these prospective partners, he wished he would see a hint of jealousy in Simone's eyes. But he never did. They were always cold, blue, bemused.

* * *

Tony had tried to do the right thing. He'd contacted the hospital complaints officer, who advised him to send an email. He got Luca to help him set up an email account. He chose the name TonyBulldogs after his favourite footy team. He wanted TonyFerrari, but it was taken. As was TonyFerrari_1, TonyFerrari_2, TonyFerrari_3 and so on. There were, as his grandson had pointed out, a million Tony Ferraris in the world.

The next night Tony got Carla to help him compose a letter. She wrote his words in her elegant cursive hand and their son Mario typed it into the computer. Tony was happy with the final result. It was polite without being pathetic, firm without being rude. When Tony pressed the send button, he felt a satisfying swell of accomplishment. That's how you have to deal with these people, he told himself. You have to play them at their own game. He knew from his years of working at a big organisation that management couldn't ignore a written document. There were certain *procedures* that had to be observed.

But weeks had passed and Tony's email inbox remained empty. 'These things take time,' Carla said when he complained, which just infuriated him even more. It suddenly struck Tony that his wife was an observer of life rather than a participant in it. Lately, the calm and patient temperament he had once so admired in her only served to exasperate him. For the first time in forty years, Tony fantasised about how his life might have turned out if he'd married feisty Gabriella from high school.

He thought of Luca's poster. He remembered the way the family had shut Luca down, how Mario had scolded his son for being antisocial and aggressive. At the time, Tony had agreed with them, but now he saw that his grandson was the voice of reason. Ever since he was three years old, Luca had been calling injustice as he saw it. *That's not fair!* he would scream when he didn't get his turn on the swings at the playground, and Tony would promise him an ice-cream if he would just let the obnoxious kid with braces have one more go. But his grandson was right. They could all learn something from the boy's fearlessness. Tony recalled the expert way Luca had gutted a garfish on their last fishing trip to Queenscliff. He hadn't stopped until the dirty job was finished—hadn't even flinched.

* * *

A couple of weeks after the poster incident, Simone called Deepak into her office. He wasn't worried—the last time she'd summoned him like this, she'd kissed him violently against the filing cabinet. But this time when he walked through the door, Simone had a serious face.

'There's been a complaint,' she said as he pulled the door closed behind him. She sat down and pointed to a document on her desk.

It was an email addressed to the hospital complaints officer. As Deepak read it, words bounded off the page: *Rude. Abrupt. Uncaring.* He looked at the name at the bottom. Tony Ferrari. It took Deepak a while to recall the patient. Mid-fifties, maybe. A drinker's nose. A rugged, fleshy face.

'It's dated the eighth of March,' he said, flicking the paper back across the desk. 'Why am I only seeing this now?'

'You know what HR's like,' Simone said and shook her head. 'There was Easter, and then Anzac Day. They've been sitting on this thing for weeks.'

Deepak sat down in the chair opposite her.

'I pulled the file,' she said. 'All you've written is: *Query nerve damage. Trial Lyrica. Discharge from clinic.*'

Now he remembered. The guy had sustained a tibial fracture after falling off a broken ladder. The X-rays looked great, but he'd developed chronic pain from a nerve injury. Simone's face was poker-like, professional.

'Do you think it's him?' Deepak asked.

She raised her eyebrows. She had forgotten. Already.

'The poster.'

'Oh. That.' She rubbed her forehead. 'God, I don't know.

Probably.' For once she looked tired. Older. 'You'll have to write a response. Acknowledging without apologising.'

Deepak groaned.

Simone sat up tall and taut again. 'We spoke to some of the nurses who were at the clinic the day you saw him.'

Now it was Deepak's turn to raise his eyebrows.

'It's protocol,' she said.

'And?' Deepak felt confident of his relationship with the nurses. He was always respectful and courteous to them.

'The unit manager said you were patronising.'

The blood drained from Deepak's face.

'But she acknowledged it could be cultural.'

That night Deepak sat down at the dining table in his St Kilda Road apartment to compose his letter. He swirled the scotch in his glass, savoured the crisp tinkle of ice cubes. He put the glass down and stared at the computer screen. After five minutes he leant back in his chair and poured himself another shot. Through the floor-to-ceiling windows, the Shrine of Remembrance glowed gold.

Deepak had bought the apartment from the parents of a doctor friend. It had been a private sale, without agents, conducted over a meal of salmon and champagne. After dessert, his friend's father, a jeweller, had shown Deepak his briefcase of diamonds. There was still an industrial-grade safe bolted to the floor of the walk-in wardrobe, empty now except for Deepak's watch and passport.

Deepak looked around the room. With the help of his sister, he had made the place inviting. A Natuzzi couch, an impractical coffee table, a couple of tastefully mismatched cushions. Friends who'd bought their own places had assured Deepak that when he found his future home he would *just know*. It was like love, they said, all heart and no head. Deepak had convinced himself he loved the apartment, the opulence of it: the soft-closing drawers, the black timber joinery, the luxurious Italian carpet. But the more time he spent at Simone's place, with its hand-picked art and fresh flowers, the more he thought his flat looked like an apartment for rent on Airbnb.

He glared at the blinking cursor. What was it Simone had said? Acknowledge without apologising? *Dear Tony*, he wrote and immediately felt a sharp pang of resentment. It wasn't his fault the old man had climbed up a broken ladder, or that he'd developed chronic nerve pain as a result of his injury. If Deepak had been rude that day in outpatients, it was probably because he'd been working straight through since the night before without a break, or because his registrar had called in sick, or because he'd had to plough through the thirty-plus patients the nurses had squeezed into an overbooked clinic.

Mr Ferrari, he typed. *Life sucks. Shit happens. This time it happened to you.*

* * *

Once, a while ago now, Tony had held his head high like the doctor. He'd been proud of his success. Everything he owned, from their four-bedroom bungalow to the antique jewellery in Carla's dresser, was a direct result of his sweat and hard work. God knows how many hours he had spent chatting footy with people he hated as he made his way from factory worker to line manager and finally to operations director. But it was worth it. The day he got that promotion was still one of the best days of his life. He would never forget the delighted looks on the faces of Carla and the boys when he brought home four air tickets to the Gold Coast.

But it hadn't lasted. And though Tony took credit for every step forward he'd taken, he didn't feel like he'd played any part in his own downfall. After the global financial crisis, the board sold the company to a multinational. Tony and all of middle management were made redundant in the restructure. Tony's position had literally vanished before his eyes—one day his name was in a little yellow box on the company's organisational flow chart, and the next day his name and the little yellow box were gone. He was three days shy of his sixtieth birthday when he filled a cardboard box with pens and photo frames from his desk. Sixty was a terrible age to be looking for a job. Especially for Tony, who had worked his way up through the ranks at a time when experience and street smarts trumped a university degree.

People in the company had looked up to him, even admired him, but that meant nothing now.

Tony lasted ten minutes in the queue at Centrelink. He had expected junkies, people with tiny pupils and needle marks on their arms, but in reality there were a lot of middle-aged men who looked just like him. Depressed. Despondent. Defeated. He felt sick. He walked out through the sliding glass doors and never went back.

Instead, he started doing odd jobs for his neighbours. Old women, mainly. He mowed Miss Howard's lawn. He installed Ikea cabinets in Mrs Ferragamo's laundry. Tony was good with his hands and the work was satisfying—and the undeclared, tax-free cash didn't hurt either. He and Carla even managed to get away to Daylesford for a long weekend, which was something they'd never done while Tony was working. By the time the redundancy money ran out, they'd almost paid off the mortgage.

Tony was feeling positive about the future the day Mrs Jackman asked him to clean her gutters. It was a cloudless day in February, the sun bright overhead. He'd completed three jobs in the morning and his wallet was fat with cash. Mrs Jackman was ninety-two. Everything in her house was old and broken. Tony should have known better than to use her ladder to climb up onto the roof, but she had caught him on his way home, and he was in a hurry—Carla had asked if they could have lunch together at the shopping centre that afternoon.

Mrs Jackman's tabby hissed ominously as Tony leant the ladder against the wall. He only made it to the second rung before the whole thing collapsed beneath him. When Tony heard the snap, he couldn't be sure if it was the sound of the ladder breaking or his leg. He soon found out that it was both. Mrs Jackman called 000, and the ambulance arrived in less than ten minutes.

The doctors said it was a straightforward fracture. A crack at the top of his shinbone, just inside the knee joint. If he were younger they might consider operating, but at Tony's age a cast would do. Six weeks, they said, and he'd be right as rain. Worst-case scenario, he might need a few weeks of physio.

The first month went according to plan, but during the fifth week the foot sticking out the bottom of the cast had swelled to the size of a small watermelon. The pain was unbearable. When the emergency doctor sawed off the plaster, Tony winced at the sight of his leg—a foul-smelling log of maroon flesh.

The doctors couldn't explain it. At first they suspected a blood clot, but the ultrasound of Tony's blood vessels was normal. Unable to walk or drive, Tony had no option but to lie in bed and watch the telly. Over the next few months, in spite of multiple X-rays and CT scans that proved the fracture was healing, Tony's condition deteriorated. When he looked at his leg—fat and useless and propped up on a mound of pillows—it looked like it belonged to someone else. Someone fat, ruddy, unhealthy. The unhealthiness was like a cancer, spreading from his one sick appendage to his entire body, until one day Tony didn't recognise the sad, bloated face in the mirror.

'You're depressed,' his GP declared, as if she had cracked a puzzle. Tony nodded. The GP gave him options, but Tony wasn't in the mood for making decisions. In his melancholic state, every road seemed like a dead end. Eventually, after many awkward consultations, he had agreed to a plan. He would start a low-dose antidepressant and try a few sessions of counselling.

The counsellor was like the GP, kind and well meaning. Sometimes Tony said he felt better just to spare himself the disappointment in her lovely eyes. But nothing helped. The medication made him feel weird, empty. He took ten tablets before chucking the rest in the bin. He continued with the counselling because it felt good to speak to a pretty girl for half an hour once a month, but it was like a massage for the soul and, like any massage, its effects were not long-lasting. As soon as he walked out the door, his leg burned and throbbed just as badly as it had before.

When summer rolled around again, the heat made the pain worse, and when Tony wore shorts to the supermarket people gaped at his pink hairless leg. Rather than go out, he spent days drifting in and out of sleep on the couch. In

January the occupational therapist recommended that Tony use a walking stick to help with his balance. Carla picked up extra cleaning shifts at the nursing home to pay off the last of the mortgage. And then, on the anniversary of the accident, something in Tony snapped.

'Did you know it's been exactly one year since I fractured my knee?' he said, chucking the newspaper across the table.

Carla, sensing a storm on the horizon, continued washing pots in the sink. In a way she was relieved. She'd been waiting months for this to happen.

'A year today since I agreed to clean Mrs Jackman's gutters.' Tony got up and limped around the kitchen. 'She never even paid me. Never even sent a card.'

Carla said nothing. She certainly wasn't going to point out that Mrs Jackman couldn't write after her stroke, or that Tony had never actually started the job, let alone finished it. She kept on with the washing-up.

'Twelve months since that doctor in emergency said I'd be right as rain in six weeks. Right as rain? *Right as rain?* What does that even mean?'

Carla wiped her hands on her apron. She pulled two mugs down from the cupboard. 'Cup of tea?'

'You know what I reckon?'

Carla turned on the kettle, and the water began to bubble and hiss.

'I reckon somebody fucked up.'

The kettle grew louder.

'Who?' Carla asked.

'One of those teenage doctors at the hospital. They should have operated on me. They put the cast on too tight.'

Carla poured boiling water onto tea bags, watched the colourless liquid stain a dirty brown. Tony sat back down at the table and propped his leg up on a chair. There were three seats at the kitchen table nowadays. One for Tony, one for Carla and one for Tony's leg.

'This,' he said pointing to his limb, red and shiny and smooth. 'This is somebody's fault.'

Tony got an appointment with his GP that afternoon. Carla drove him to the clinic. The doctor smiled sweetly at them, totally unprepared for trouble as they walked through her door.

'I want you to refer me back to the hospital,' Tony said, his voice belligerent, before he had even sat down.

'Okay,' the doctor said, surprised at his ferocity and not wanting to provoke him further. She started typing.

Tony was itching for a fight. 'Don't you want to know why?'

She stopped what she was doing and swivelled her chair to face him. 'Tell me.'

'Today's the one-year anniversary of my accident.'

The GP nodded.

'And I'm no better.'

The doctor wheeled her chair closer to Tony. She leaned in with a concerned face.

'If anything, I'm worse,' he said.

'I know you have a lot of pain.'

'Nothing you've ever done has helped me.'

The doctor winced, and Tony felt bad. She had only ever been gentle with him.

'I'm on your side, Tony,' the doctor said.

'I know.'

'So let's write this letter.'

As the doctor typed, Tony studied Carla, sitting on a chair in the corner. She smiled encouragingly.

Weeks had passed while they waited for the hospital to make contact. Tony's anger waxed and waned. Once or twice, pottering around in the shed, he had looked at his dad's hunting rifle and thought about killing himself. He mentioned it to the counsellor, who told him that if he ever had those sort of thoughts again, he should call Lifeline immediately. She wrote the number in red pen on the back of one of her business cards.

Finally a letter arrived notifying Tony of his appointment date. Amazingly—maybe because his adrenaline levels were sky-high—the pain wasn't bad the morning of his appointment. Tony considered cancelling, but then he saw

Carla, wearing a pretty dress and a hopeful face, and he knew he had to go through with it.

As expected, he and Carla spent two hours in outpatients, waiting to see the doctor, flicking through three-year-old copies of the *Women's Weekly*, looking at the people around them and guessing who would be called next. Every so often a doctor would walk briskly past the waiting area, and the patients—growing ever more wan and listless under the fluorescent lights—would follow them with earnest eyes. But the doctors were like workhorses with blinkers, brutally focused on the task ahead. They poked their heads through doors, called names in curt voices and panned unseeingly across the sea of faces. To be fair, the doctors looked tired too. Their hair was oily and limp and their shirts were soft and crumpled. Only one doctor, a lady, looked immaculate—her navy suit shiny and pressed, her blond hair pulled into a bun.

Tony didn't hear the doctor call his name. It was Carla who dug her nails into his thigh and told him to get up. By the time Tony had hobbled into the room, the surgeon—a tall, brown-skinned man with pointy shoes—was already at his desk, glowering at the computer.

'I'm not sure why you're here,' he said when Tony and Carla sat down.

'The GP should've written a letter,' Carla said and smiled.

The doctor pulled a piece of paper from a manila folder, presumably Tony's medical file. He read the letter and leant back in the swivel chair, stretching its plastic spine almost to breaking point.

'It should all be there. In the letter,' Tony said.

'This is a fracture clinic,' the doctor replied, turning back to face his computer. 'We deal with fractures.'

Tony could feel a cold burn, like ice on a wound, around his knee. 'I *have* a fracture.'

'You *had* a fracture,' the doctor replied and pointed a finger at the computer screen in front of him. 'Your X-rays look great.'

Tony looked at the long white shadows on the black screen. They did look great—smooth and straight. He felt stupid. Like he used to feel at school when he answered a question only to have the teacher explain in front of the entire class why he was wrong.

'But my husband has a lot of pain,' Carla said.

Tony glared at her.

'Then you should be at the pain clinic,' the doctor said.

This struck Tony as the sort of simplistic explanation you might offer a small child. If you have pain, you go to the pain clinic. If you have problems with your poo, you go to the poo clinic.

'Somebody fucked up,' Tony said, glad to see Carla and the surgeon flinch. 'You say you fixed me, but instead of feeling better, I feel worse. Terrible. *Suicidal.*'

The surgeon changed his tone then. He looked nervous,

and started using words like *unforeseeable* and *regrettable*. But it was too late. Tony's eyes found the lanyard around his neck.

'Deepak,' he said. 'What is that? Indian?'

That was one step too far for the surgeon. He stopped grovelling. His momentarily pleading eyes became cold again.

'I'll write a letter to your GP. Explaining everything.'

Tony stood up. Carla handed him his stick. Tony slapped it away.

'I'll write a letter too,' he said under his breath as he limped from the room.

* * *

At the end of May, Deepak flew to the Sunshine Coast to meet Priya. Priya was twenty-eight and worked part-time as an ultrasonographer in Caloundra. She was born in Brisbane, but her father, like Deepak's parents, came from New Delhi. Deepak's mother had arranged a lunch by the beach so that they might *get to know each other better.*

There was nobody in the taxi queue at the airport in Maroochydore. Deepak threw his bag into the boot of the first cab.

'Where you headed?' the driver asked with a strong Australian accent.

'Noosa.'

They sped off. On the radio, a woman was interviewing

Bindi Irwin. Even though the DJ had just wished the daughter of the Crocodile Hunter a happy eighteenth birthday, Deepak couldn't help but picture a young blond girl in pigtails and khaki clothes. As they drove, he imagined what it must have been like growing up at Australia Zoo. He tried to picture his ten-year-old self riding the corrugated backs of crocodiles and play-fighting with kangaroos.

Priya had reserved a table on the deck with a clear view of the ocean. When Deepak arrived she was already there, sipping a drink, waiting for him. She had her back turned, but the little of her that Deepak could see looked promising. Glossy hair. Pink toenails. A long, loose summer dress. He touched her lightly on the shoulder. Her skin was warm and soft.

'You found me,' she said, turning around. Apart from a large pimple on her chin that she had tried, unsuccessfully, to cover with make-up, she was stunning. 'But then again, I am the only brown-skinned woman in the restaurant.'

Deepak laughed. He sat down in the chair beside her. They stared at the people on the beach, kids playing in the water.

'What are you drinking?' he asked.

'A lychee martini,' Priya replied. She picked up the thin-stemmed glass, inspected the liquid in it. 'But what I really want is a beer.'

Deepak laughed again. The ice had been broken. They spoke of travel and books and movies. They bonded over their disappointment with Prague and their love of Leonardo DiCaprio's movie *Inception*. Deepak did an impression of his mother. Priya imitated her dad. They argued about who did the best Indian accent. They criticised the food. Deepak's burger was too small, Priya's barramundi overcooked. They drank. They laughed. They relaxed. The conversation turned to work, and to Priya's experiences with doctors while she was being trained at the hospital. That was when she mentioned Simone.

'Actually, you might know her,' Priya said. 'I'm not sure what hospital she's at now, but apparently she's some big shot in Melbourne.'

Deepak drank from his pint. 'I may have heard of her.'

'She was a junior consultant at Royal Brisbane while I was doing my placement.'

Deepak tried to picture Simone as a junior consultant—pandering to heads of department, ingratiating herself in the presence of scrub nurses—but he couldn't.

'She's a real piece of work, that woman.'

Deepak watched a seagull attack a chip beneath the table.

'This one time, I was doing an X-ray for her in theatre—a reduction of a hip that had gone terribly wrong—and she told me my breathing was too noisy.'

Deepak feigned a look of shock. He knew from personal

experience that when Simone was stressed, which was fortunately not often, she was vicious.

'I had a cold.'

Deepak shook his head, trying to appear incredulous.

'She's a doctor. She's supposed to be compassionate.'

Deepak wanted to explain to Priya that Simone was not a doctor in the traditional sense of the word. She was not a smiling GP, plump from the chocolates her patients had given her for Christmas. She was an orthopaedic surgeon— one of only a few women in a club full of men with God complexes—and her steely demeanour was not a choice but a matter of necessity. But he didn't have the energy.

The waiter arrived with dessert menus. Priya looked at Deepak expectantly. Deepak pointed to his watch and said that he really should get going. He asked for the bill before tossing another chip to the hungry seagull between his feet.

When Deepak turned on his phone in Melbourne, he was pleased to see a message from Simone: *Come over.*

He went straight from the airport to her apartment, in a taxi. He found her in a silk robe, curled like a cat on her leather lounge. He hung his jacket on the hatstand and sat down beside her.

'How was it?'

She always said this after his meetings, always said *it*

instead of *she*. Deepak hoped this spoke to some unacknowledged, deep-seated jealousy.

'Don't be like that,' he said and slipped his hand into the open neck of her robe.

Simone pulled away and sat up straight. 'There have been more. Posters, I mean. Everybody's talking about them.'

Deepak felt his heart skip a beat.

'I thought your apology would help, but it's only made things worse.'

He thought of the letter, its final wording edited by Simone and the complaints officer. *I'm sorry this has happened to you. It was an unfortunate series of regrettable but unforeseeable events.* It was the language of government agencies and eviction notices and redundancy letters. Deepak could see how it might inflame someone.

'Is that why you asked me to come over?'

'Yes.' Simone wrapped her robe tight around her chest. 'I've spoken to others in the department, and we all agree that it would be best for you to take some time off. Until this thing blows over.'

Deepak stood up. He put on his jacket. It didn't matter that he was in a suit and Simone was in a robe—he knew who held the power.

'Well, if you all agree.'

Even now he wished that she would grab his arm, implore him to stay—something. He would forgive her everything.

But Simone didn't even get up off the couch. She remained seated, statuesque.

Deepak had a cousin, Jignesh, who was a lawyer. They met for a coffee in the Royal Arcade building.

'Can you prove this Tony guy put up the posters?' Jignesh asked. 'Are there CCTV cameras in the car park?'

Deepak scooped the foam off his cappuccino. 'I don't know. I don't think so.'

'So all you've got is a hunch?'

'Pretty much.'

Deepak looked at the sheen on his cousin's tailor-made suit. He felt self-conscious and underdressed. He'd only been off work for two days but had already resorted to ripped jeans and a footy jumper.

'My best advice is to ignore it. These things blow over.'

'That's what my boss said.'

'Well, your boss is a smart man.' Jignesh looked at his watch, jiggling his leg beneath the table.

'I'll pay for the coffees,' Deepak said. 'You should go.'

'Thanks, man.' Jignesh looked relieved as he stood up. He slapped Deepak's shoulder. 'Remember when we were kids and we sculled shots of Sambuca in your garage?'

'Yeah.'

'I miss those days.'

'Me too.'

Deepak watched his cousin's black head disappear into the lunchtime throng. He paid the waitress—who had flirted outrageously with Jignesh but refused to make eye contact with Deepak—and wandered through Bourke Street Mall. On the tram, he scoured the unnervingly familiar faces of the passengers. An old woman in a pink scarf who might have had a hip replacement. A pretty redhead Deepak might have admitted, once, for septic arthritis. A tradie with a tribal tattoo whose leg Deepak might have plastered. Everybody was a suspect.

Weeks passed with no word from Simone. Deepak watched his annual leave dwindle on his pay slip. He was nothing without work. He was not sporty. He was not creative. He had few friends—most of whom were doctors and worked just as hard as he did. At first Deepak devoted entire days to Facebook, but after a while the photos of other people's holidays made him sick. He moved on to watching back-to-back episodes of *Making a Murderer* and searching the internet for the porn star who most resembled Simone.

For once he was pleased when his sister, Monisha, phoned. It was ten pm and he was in bed with his laptop.

'What's up?' he asked.

He waited for her to launch into some tirade about their parents—the only reason, these days, that Monisha seemed to call him. He wondered what it would be this time—their mother criticising her cooking, their father pressuring her to have another son. But it was neither.

'It's Mum,' Monisha said, her voice faltering. 'She's in hospital.'

When Deepak arrived, around eleven, his mother was sitting in bed, smiling. 'Such a terrible, terrible pain, Deepak.'

Deepak picked up the observation chart. She was afebrile. Her ECG was okay. Her blood pressure and heart rate were within normal limits. She certainly looked well, with bright eyes and waves of glossy hair. If anything, it was Deepak's father who seemed under the weather, slumped in the corner, his skin tinted grey by the fluorescent lights.

'What happened?'

'Your mother was doing too much. As usual.'

'I wouldn't have to do so much, if your father would just help out a little.' Much to Deepak's surprise, his mother looked delighted with her situation.

'Vacuuming? At nine o'clock at night?' his father persisted.

'Monisha was going to bring the children in the morning.'

'The children would only mess it up again.'

'I can't sleep in a dirty house.'

'I told you to hire someone.'

'I don't want some stranger rifling through my underwear. I just want my lazy husband to get off his bottom.'

'I'm too old.'

'And what do you think I am?' Deepak's mother said, pointing down at her gowned belly and stockinged feet. 'A spring chicken?'

Deepak couldn't take it anymore and held up his hands. 'Please. Mum. Dad. Just tell me what happened.'

His mother launched into a needlessly detailed account of her day. She had first noticed the chest pain while preparing his father's dinner. The pain had grown worse when her sister from London called to brag about her renovations. 'But the final straw,' she said, waving her finger in the air, 'was when Mr Peterson told me he had seen a poster of you at the hospital.'

Deepak felt his cheeks burn. Luckily his parents' elderly neighbour, Mr Peterson, was not a reliable witness.

'Imagine! A poster saying my son is a bad doctor. My son! A bad doctor!' She clutched her chest.

Deepak's father jumped in. 'That man has always been jealous of us. He only has one daughter and she never visits him.'

'I think he might be getting dementia,' his mother said.

Deepak sighed.

'Anyway, I blame Mr Peterson for this chest pain.' Deepak's mother massaged her breastbone. 'If I die, you can sue him.'

'You're not dying, Mum.'

'I should hope not. I told the doctor I'm not ready.' She stared at Deepak with defiant eyes. 'I told him I had to stay alive to see my only son have children.'

*

It was three am by the time Deepak left the hospital. The blood results had come back: his mother had *not* had a heart attack. The doctors said her chest pains were probably the result of acid reflux, or muscle strain, or stress. Exhausted, he sat in the front seat of his Porsche, revving the engine and staring at the bright red emergency sign.

Deepak didn't see the boy at first. It was only when his eyes adjusted to the dark that he noticed the teenager, hoodie pulled low over his eyes, hiding behind a pillar while a heavily pregnant woman and her partner made their way to their car. When the coast was clear, the boy sprinted towards the hospital's emergency entrance and rummaged in his pockets, pulling out a piece of paper and sticking it to the sliding glass door. Deepak gripped the steering wheel. He watched the boy run back to the pillar again and then scamper towards a Holden Commodore. Deepak was only metres away—he could see the shadow of another person in the driver's seat.

He started the Porsche and rolled forwards, straight towards the Holden, blocking the way so it couldn't pull out, and then killed the engine. The driver hadn't even had time to put the key in the ignition. Deepak stepped out of his car, his rubber shoes squelching on the wet concrete. He was determined to resolve this matter once and for all. He felt the flare of the Holden's high beams on his face and waited for something to happen.

* * *

Tony didn't recognise the man in the beanie who emerged from the sleek black car. At first he thought it might be an undercover policeman, but Tony had never heard of a policeman driving a Porsche. Luca was fidgeting on the seat beside him. Tony felt an ache in his chest and took a few sprays from his Anginine pump.

'Fuck!' said Luca.

'Relax.'

'It's him.'

'Who?' Tony peered through the windscreen at the man, who was shielding his face with his hand.

'The doctor.'

Tony examined the man again. Luca was right. He looked different in normal clothes—Tony had only seen him in a suit—but there was no mistaking the expensive watch and the cocky way he stood, as if the world owed him something.

Luca laughed. He was enjoying this. Tony didn't like to admit it, but there was something not quite right about his grandson. Every chance he got, Tony warned the boy off drugs. He suspected a hit of ice would be just the thing to unhinge him.

'Look at his car,' Luca said, and again Tony did as he was told. Anything was better than looking at Luca, smiling and salivating like a predator on the seat beside him.

'Probably bought it with the money he made fucking you over.'

Tony nodded, but as he watched the doctor blinking in the headlights—reduced to a human being by the beanie and the tracksuit pants—he felt the rage he had maintained for so long desert him. Tony reached for the handle of the car door. He was ready to make peace with the guy. But he was too slow. Luca jumped out first. Tony saw his grandson's hooded face through the windshield. He felt his heart pound against his ribs. He watched the doctor stab the air with his finger and Luca's soft lips curl into a snarl. He heard himself gasp and a voice, very much like his own but different somehow, mutter *No, no, no, no, no!*

Tony had given Luca the knife as a gift one weekend at Lake Eildon. He had shown Luca how to use it on the sequined skin of a rainbow trout—shown him how to slash the fish's belly in one quick move before scooping its guts out with his bare hands. There was no mistaking it—the bright green handle, the curved blade flashing white in the glare of the Holden's headlights. The surgeon—a man familiar with knives and scalpels—saw it too. He backed away.

It was fast and it was gruesome—a couple of quick thrusts. Tony watched the body writhing on the ground as blood hosed, like black oil, across the concrete.

Within seconds Luca was back in the car, hot and breathless.

'You idiot,' Tony said, with a calm that surprised him. 'Give it to me.'

Luca handed over the knife, red and wet and sticky.

'Go,' Tony said.

But Luca didn't move. He was like a child, waiting for his nonno to punish him.

'Go!'

Luca ran away from the car, hesitantly at first, and then at great speed, his hair flapping wildly.

Tony got out of the Holden. He looked down at the doctor, heaving in a pool of blood at his feet. He looked straight ahead at the flickering red emergency sign. He looked up at the dome of sky, at the stars glinting overhead. He crossed himself. *In the name of the Father, and the Son, and the Holy Ghost...*

Toy Town

Maha despised the play centre. It smelled faintly of soiled nappies, and her four-year-old daughter, Amani, always found a sultana at the bottom of the ball pit. But Amani loved the curly blue slide, and it got them out of the house. With all the rain this winter, they had been spending a lot of time at home lately and the claustrophobia was driving them crazy.

It was Maha's fourth winter in Melbourne, but it felt as cold and lonely as her first. Maybe more so, because this year Malik was working three out of five days in Sydney. Maha had thought she would feel settled by now, that she would at least have a couple of friends. But the only people she spent any time with were Malik's elderly parents. Last year she had gone for a couple of coffees with a Ukrainian woman from her English class, but when the six-week course ended, they had lost touch.

Having a child was isolating. Days were lost in a haze of housework and playdough and preparation of snacks. In Beirut, Maha would have had a maid—a girl from Sri Lanka, probably—to help with the household chores, which would free her up to do some teaching, maybe have her hair done at the salon. At four years of age, Amani would already be at school, learning to read and write and count, instead of spending just a few days a week at kindergarten, painting with her fingers and making cakes in the sandpit.

There were two people in the high-ceilinged room when they arrived, a Caucasian woman with red hair and a girl who looked the same age as Amani. The girl was in the toddler area, feeding pretend food to a one-eyed teddy bear. Maha ordered a cappuccino and sat down at a table near the back of the room. Amani immediately flicked off her shoes and ran towards the curly blue slide. She scaled the padded ramp with ease, in spite of the slipperiness of her socks.

Maha scooped milk froth into her mouth. She did love the coffee in Melbourne. The cappuccinos were a wonderful compromise between Lebanese coffee and the freeze-dried Nescafé she drank back home. As Amani explored, Maha held the warm mug up to her cheek and checked her phone. There was a message from Malik. It said *miss you* in Arabic letters with a red heart emoji. There was a photo from her mother, too—a picture of her four aunts, all made up for her cousin's wedding.

After a month in Melbourne, Maha had stopped caring about her appearance. It seemed absurd to spend two hours doing her make-up only to go to the supermarket, where everybody had their wrinkles and pimples on show. How Maha's mother would cringe if she saw her now—wearing an old hijab, scuffed leather shoes and just a hint of eyeliner. And while Maha did miss spending hours having her nails done with her mum at the salon, there was something freeing about getting ready in twenty minutes—not having to worry about being caught out by a relative at the local coffee shop without her three-inch heels.

Her mother still called her every night, worried, asking if she'd made any friends. Though Malik insisted that Australia was a tolerant place, Maha's mother was fearful. She'd read the articles in the newspapers, seen the riots on TV. When Maha and Malik got engaged, Malik assured his future mother-in-law he lived in a good Melbourne suburb—full of progressive, left-leaning Aussies. Sure enough, Maha's experiences of outright racism had been few and far between. There was the boy who'd left a flyer on her car windscreen that said *ISIS terrorist go home*, and the local handyman who'd refused to mow her lawn, but mostly the Australians she met were well-intentioned. After flinching—almost imperceptibly—at the sight of Maha's hijab, they smiled and tried to ingratiate themselves to alleviate their guilt about their initial reaction. Maha didn't begrudge them this. When she'd first arrived in Melbourne she had judged her neighbours harshly too, for their unkempt hair and their sleeve tattoos and the ladders in their stockings.

Maha saw the woman with the red hair look back in her direction. It was an awkward move. A hello but not a hello. Maha felt Amani at her elbow, tugging on her blouse and asking for water. Maha gave her the *Frozen* water bottle she always carried in her handbag.

'There's another girl here,' Amani whispered in Arabic.

'You should go and talk to her,' Maha said.

Amani cocked her head to the side, stuck out her bottom lip. 'Will you come with me?'

Maha sighed. She put her phone in her bag and stood up. Happy, Amani ran towards the girl, who was still absorbed in her tea party.

'Can I play with you?' Maha heard her daughter ask in English. She didn't hear the girl's reply, but it must have been yes, because the next minute they were taking turns to cuddle the one-eyed teddy.

Maha stood, stranded, halfway between her table and the toddler area. The red-headed woman was perched on a bench with her back to Maha, watching the two girls. Maha looked at the old man who took the money and made the coffees, but he was busy typing something on his phone. She could easily retreat to her seat and catch up on the Lebanese news online, but something about the way the mother was sitting, with her spine straight and taut, told Maha she anticipated a conversation. Maha shuffled forwards a little, pretending to watch Amani. Bored of the teddy, the girls were now diving off the plastic slide into the pit of brightly coloured balls. Their shrieks echoed around the room.

When Maha sat down on the bench, the woman looked at her and smiled.

'It's easy when they find a friend.'

'Yes.'

'Charlotte loves it here.'

Maha looked at Charlotte, rolling in a sea of balls.

'My daughter, Amani, loves it too.'

Charlotte's mother looked towards the old man at the front counter and lowered her voice. 'But I can't stand the place.'

Maha laughed. 'Me too!'

'There aren't any windows.'

'Yes!'

'And it smells.'

'Yes!'

The old man looked in their direction then, which only made them giggle even more.

'I'm Nicole,' Charlotte's mother said, holding out her

hand. Maha shook it. The woman's skin was rough and dry.

'I'm Maha.'

'That's a beautiful name.'

'Thank you.'

Maha wondered if she should return the compliment, but the moment had passed.

Charlotte ran up and started clawing at Nicole's bag. 'I'm hungry.' The little girl had dark hair and brown eyes and looked nothing like her mother.

'Charlotte takes after her father,' Nicole said, as if reading Maha's mind. 'He eats like a horse too.' She pulled a Tupperware box from her bag and opened it. Charlotte took out a small, deep-fried ball and sunk her teeth into it. A shower of crumbs fell to the floor.

'Falafel,' Nicole said and smiled proudly. 'I made them myself.'

Maha inspected the golden-brown balls. They vaguely resembled the falafel she knew, only drier, and slightly burnt.

'My father worked in Saudi Arabia when I was young,' Nicole explained. 'We travelled a lot.'

Maha was surprised. She would never have guessed that someone who looked like Nicole had lived in the Middle East.

'I'm from Lebanon,' Maha said.

'I love Lebanon!'

Maha saw Amani abandon the ball pit and sidle up beside her new friend. When Nicole held out the lunch box, Amani screwed up her face and shook her head.

Nicole smiled and turned back to Maha. 'I love Baalbek, and the Bekaa Valley and the cedar forests in the mountains.'

Maha nodded, stunned that this woman, with her strong Australian accent and freckled skin, could know her country so intimately.

'I'm hungry too,' Amani declared.

Maha dug inside her tote for the sandwich bag she had packed in a hurry that morning. She felt self-conscious as she passed the three chocolate biscuits and white bread sandwich to her daughter in front of Nicole. They suddenly seemed too processed, too unimaginative, too mainstream.

'Is that yummy?' Nicole asked as Amani took alternate bites of the chocolate biscuit she held in one hand and the sandwich she held in the other.

Amani nodded.

Nicole smiled. 'What have you got inside your sandwich today?'

'Vegemite,' Amani replied. A small piece of wet bread fell from her lips onto the floor.

'She loves Vegemite,' Maha said, leaning down and picking it up.

'How funny,' Nicole laughed. 'Charlotte and I can't stand the stuff!'

Charlotte thrust a half-eaten falafel into Nicole's hand and wiped her lips with the back of her sleeve. She took

Amani's hand and pointed to the bouncy castle. Amani looked at Maha, her big brown eyes pleading. Maha nodded and the girls ran off, leaving her in a scatter of falafel crumbs and sandwich crusts.

'How do you find it here, in Melbourne?' Nicole asked. She buried the Tupperware inside her bag.

Maha thought of the street they lived on, its crumbling weatherboard houses, the word *WHORE!* scrawled across a block of units with an arrow pointing to some poor person's front door. But she wanted to be kind to Nicole's home country, just as Nicole had been kind to hers.

'It's beautiful,' she said.

'Mummy, watch this!' Charlotte yelled. She did a handstand in the bouncy castle. Nicole waved and clapped her hands to show she was impressed.

'It must be hard, though,' Nicole said when Charlotte turned away. She said it with such sincerity that Maha wondered if she spoke from experience—beyond that of a child expat spending school holidays in a compound in Saudi Arabia.

'It is difficult,' Maha said, recalling the first night she'd spent alone in her Australian home—her bed vibrating with the booming music from a nearby house party as she obsessed about the flimsiness of the front fence. She had longed for the safety of her parents' Beirut apartment with its wrought-iron gates and concrete walls and security guard at the front door.

She was still racking her brain for the right words to describe it all when she saw Nicole snatch a look at her watch.

'We'd better get going,' Nicole said, standing up. 'I have to go to the supermarket.'

'Yes, me too,' Maha said, even though she had done her shopping yesterday.

Nicole told Charlotte to put on her sneakers, and Charlotte dropped to the ground, yelling, 'No!' When Nicole insisted, her daughter screamed until her face burned red, and yellow snot poured out of her nose. After ten minutes of shouting and pleading, Charlotte finally agreed to put on her shoes in return for a biscuit and five minutes on the iPad when she got home.

They walked out of the Toy Town play centre together, all four of them. Outside, the two girls ran ahead.

'It was nice to meet you,' Maha said.

'Same here.'

Maha pulled her coat tighter around her body.

'We should do this again,' Nicole said.

'Yes,' Maha agreed.

Nicole wrapped a green hand-knitted scarf around her neck. 'See you.' She didn't offer to exchange phone numbers. Maha felt disappointed, and then relieved.

'Bye.'

The girls were far ahead of them now, holding hands and skipping towards the pedestrian crossing. They looked similar from behind—the same height, with the same bouncing brown ponytails. Maha and Nicole called out, but the girls didn't hear. They were too busy laughing and singing and telling each other fanciful tales.

Doughnuts

Pandora was Barry's first client, ever. They'd met the year he graduated with a bachelor of social work from Victoria University. Back then she was stunning: dark, feline, defiant. Like Cleopatra, except with a potty-mouth. But that was ten years ago, and all the long admissions had played havoc with her. Every now and then, Barry saw a hint of her long-lost beauty—in the line of her regal nose, or her vaguely purple eyes, which Pandora likened to Elizabeth Taylor's. Despite the age difference, Barry had been attracted to her at the start. The way she'd looked at him was exhilarating, like she could tap into his core.

Pandora had been doing well recently, and Barry had cut down his visits to once a month. But last Tuesday at three am, a neighbour had called 000 about booming ABBA music, and the local police, who all knew Pandora well, had alerted Barry.

It was nine-thirty by the time Barry arrived at her weatherboard near the housing commission. Pandora's father, a hardworking pharmacist, had left her the property in his will, which—in spite of its proximity to the flats— would easily fetch $800,000. Barry was surprised Pandora had never mentioned selling it during one of her manias, but luckily simple logic often evaded her at those times.

The garden was full of weeds. Somebody had scrawled *PORK* in spiky capitals across the splintered timber fence. Piles of painted canvases were stacked on the front verandah—oils in bright primary colours, peanut butter thick. Pandora would be in the backyard, painting probably, in spite of the bitter winter weather.

Pandora was out the back, as Barry thought, but she wasn't painting. She was lying on a broken deckchair, naked, except for sunglasses and a tanning mirror open on her lap.

'Barry,' she said, as if his impromptu visit were nothing out of the ordinary. 'Sit down.'

Barry turned a milk crate upside down to make a seat. 'Top of the morning to you.'

Pandora laughed. Her flesh was a field of goosebumps. 'Glorious day, isn't it?'

Barry looked up at the sky, heavy with grey cloud.

'We've got to enjoy these last moments, Barry. Before the end.'

Barry nodded. Armageddon psychosis. There'd been a lot of it around lately.

'When Trump presses that button, we're all dead. Kaput. And the unlucky ones who survive the blast will be destroyed by their own radioactively mutated cells.'

Barry could see the shadows of veins like tangled wires beneath Pandora's skin. He pulled a picnic blanket from beneath a stack of newspapers and laid it on top of her.

'Never mind climate change,' she said and laughed. 'We'll all be dead this side of Christmas.'

As Pandora cackled about the impending apocalypse, Barry constructed a plan. First he would speak to her psychiatrist, then the crisis assessment and treatment team, and finally, as a last resort, the police, if she refused to go willingly.

'Fancy a bloody mary?' Pandora said, sitting up. Her pendulous breasts swayed, metronome-like, above her knees.

The admission was messy. Casey, the woman who arrived from the crisis team, was someone Pandora had had run-ins with before. On seeing her, Pandora-the-laughing-doomsayer was transformed into Pandora-the-spatula-wielding-assassin. Barry helped the police bundle his picnic-blanket-wrapped patient into the back of the ambulance. When they'd left, he went back inside. He plucked a jumper and a pair of leopard-print leggings from the floor and then made his way to the hospital.

Barry would never forget the time he'd called the crisis team for his father. It was a hot day in March, a few days after his dad's sixtieth birthday, and Barry and his mother had returned early from her appointment with the oncologist. The doctor had good news—her cancer had responded to the latest bout of chemotherapy. They were desperate to tell Barry's father but couldn't find him anywhere inside the house. It was Barry's mother who finally discovered him, in the garage, jamming a hose into the Holden's exhaust pipe. He'd bowed his head like a criminal as he followed her inside and didn't say a word—not when she boiled the kettle and placed a mug of tea in front of him, not when he heard Barry on the phone to psych triage, and not later, in the bathroom, when Barry cleaned the soot from his hands with a wet face cloth.

That night, as Barry locked the garden hose away in the shed, he'd kept one eye out for a note—some confession or apology or last declaration of love—but if it was there, he couldn't find it.

He sat in his car in the hospital car park. The clock read four-thirty. Pandora's admission had absorbed the entire day.

He watched a pretty woman in scrubs—a junior doctor, perhaps—check the lock on her car three, four, five times. He watched her walk halfway to the hospital front entrance before turning back to test the lock again. Barry looked down at his phone, checked his inbox. There was an email from his father's nursing home. There had been another outbreak of gastroenteritis. The last time his father got gastro, he'd ended up in hospital. Barry hadn't planned on visiting him tonight, but now he would have to, if only to pacify that niggling pain inside his chest.

The nursing home was in a trendy inner-city area—a blond brick building tucked between two cafes selling pulled-pork sliders for twenty dollars. Barry parked beside an ambulance. He wondered if it was waiting for his father, but he'd had no missed calls and the carers were pretty good with notifications. They'd rung him the time a new nurse accidentally gave his dad Miss Longbottom's medicine, and when a lady with dementia had bitten him on the thigh.

Barry found his father in a wheelchair in front of the television. *Judge Judy* was on, her voice cutting through the noise of somebody's oxygen machine. Barry couldn't tell if his father was sleeping. His eyes were half open, only the whites showing.

'Dad,' he said, placing a hand on his father's reassuringly warm arm. His father jerked awake.

'Blanche?' He sucked a tendril of saliva back into his mouth.

'Not Blanche, Dad. It's Barry.'

The old man's eyes flickered across his son's face before returning to *Judge Judy*.

'I brought you something,' Barry said, digging into his satchel and pulling out a doughnut he'd bought for lunch but hadn't had time to eat. 'Your favourite.'

The old man lifted the bag to his nose and inhaled deeply.

'Do you like this show?' Barry asked.

'It's all right.' His father shoved the doughnut into his mouth. 'She's not afraid to tell it like it is.'

Barry watched the jam spill like congealed blood from his father's lips. When the diagnosis of Alzheimer's was made, Barry had hoped his dad's heart might soften with his brain, but it hadn't. Though his memory failed and his bladder failed, his sternness never swayed. Perhaps once, a long time ago, there had been a soft centre in there somewhere, but over the years it had calcified—thickened and puckered like a scar.

Only the drink had ever worked to relax him, and then only for a short while. Barry had enjoyed those Christmas lunches when his father was loose with brandy, when he would tell them tales from Vietnam—funny stories, like how he had dared his best mate, Mike, to eat ten chillies, or how he had fallen off his motorbike into a steaming pile of buffalo dung. It'd be ten years, at least, since Barry had seen his father like that. With each passing year, his heart had hardened that little bit more—as if, like some character from Greek mythology, he was slowly being turned to stone.

Barry pulled up a chair and sat down beside his father. Judge Judy was lecturing some girl about teenage pregnancy.

Barry cleared his throat. 'I hear there's a gastro outbreak.'

'A what?' His father turned on his hearing aid, waited for the inevitable shriek.

'Diarrhoea going round.'

'Ah.'

'You okay?'

'Yep.' Doughnut sugar clung like glitter to the front of his woollen jumper. 'But poor George in room ten died from the bloody thing.'

'Really?' Barry was shocked. They hadn't mentioned *that* in the email.

'Imagine. Dying. From the runs.'

And in the weighty silence that ensued, Barry contemplated just that.

As Barry signed out of the facility, one of the nurses approached him. She had a familiar face, but he couldn't for the life of him remember her name. Just in time, his eyes found the ID badge pinned to her smallish breast.

'Olga.'

'Mr Wheeler's son. Your visits mean the world to him.'

Barry was sure she said that to the relatives of all her patients, but it was still nice to hear—to pretend, for a while.

'And he's so very proud,' she added, looking down at the faded knees of his jeans. 'He says you're a doctor?'

'Social worker,' Barry corrected her. He smiled. 'Close enough.'

The nurse laughed a loud, overcompensating laugh.

Tonight he would have to take one of the sleeping tablets rolling around in his drawer. Something about seeing his dad gave him terrible insomnia. Growing up, he had fallen asleep to the sound of his father's slippers pacing the floor. A couple of times he had buried his head in a pillow to shelter his ears from the howls. Come morning, nobody mentioned it. They all pretended it never happened. Only one time, when a neighbour complained, did Barry's mum whisper something about the war.

Barry heated up a Lite n' Easy meal in the microwave and turned on the television. He watched *MasterChef*, which only made his food even less appetising than it already was. He followed this with a beer, and then another, and another. In the end he didn't need a tablet but passed out, half-drunk, on the couch.

*

The next morning Barry was busy with other clients, and it was late afternoon by the time he got to the hospital. Pandora was in the internal courtyard, stalking back and forth and smoking. She had dressed herself in the leopard-print leggings and the long hot-pink jumper. Barry watched her, unnoticed, through the floor-to-ceiling glass doors. She was talking to somebody hidden from view behind a giant potted fern. Pandora rarely had visitors. Occasionally her cousin dropped off a pack of cigarettes out of some vague sense of familial duty, but Pandora's cousin was tall—too tall to be hidden by a fern.

Barry moved to another window to get a better look at the visitor. Even behind a veil of leaves, her resemblance to Pandora was striking. They had the same lips, the same lilac eyes, the same mane of dyed black hair. Except this woman was smooth and serious—like a wax mannequin of the real thing. Barry left the two women to talk and climbed the stairs to the cafeteria.

Four o'clock was a bad time to eat at the hospital. The chips sagged, the lettuce hung limply from the mouths of burgers, and roughly cut chunks of lamb shrivelled in swamps of curry. Barry picked up a jam doughnut, wrapped in plastic, to have with his coffee. It was stale and all the sugar rubbed off when he unwrapped it, but he ate it dutifully, because his father had taught him never to waste food, and because, for a moment, it stopped the grumble emanating from his stomach.

Doughnuts reminded Barry of his mother. Sometimes, when he was a boy, she would take him with her on the tram to Victoria Market. Barry loved all the colour and noise of the stalls, and he could touch things when nobody was looking, like the hairy, spiky skins of fruits that looked like they came from another planet. If Barry was good, his mother would buy three jam doughnuts in a brown paper bag. She and Barry would eat theirs on the ride home—still hot from the deep-fryer—as they marvelled at the lofty buildings and frantic lunchtime crowds. At home, Barry would present the last jam-filled treat to his father, on a tray, with a pot of hot tea. It might just have been the effect of Barry's cheerful mood, but on those days even his father seemed a little less formidable.

When he finally sat down with Pandora, alone, she was angry.

'What did you go and call the police for, Barry?'

It was a conversation they'd had before.

'You're getting sick again, Pandora. I did it for your own good.'

Pandora snorted through flared nostrils, flicked a lock of her tangled hair.

'Who was that lady you were speaking to before?' he asked.

'You spying on me now?' Pandora snapped. 'None of your business.'

'Was it Maria?'

Her shoulders caved, as if the mere mention of her daughter's name had wounded her.

'Like I said,' she repeated, but this time without the fire, 'none of your goddamn business.'

Barry heated up his Lite n' Easy meal, but there was no *MasterChef* tonight. It was Friday—most people were out—and the choice was between *Finding Nemo* and *Pretty Woman*. He put his DVD of *Apocalypse Now* in the DVD player. When Barry was growing up, his dad had banned them from watching movies about Vietnam. If they came on TV, he would shout, 'What a load of rubbish!' and hurl his slipper at the screen. Even as a child, Barry had wondered if all this was just an act. Perhaps, rather than a poor imitation, the films were actually too close to reality. After all, joker Mike who had eaten the chillies was eventually blown apart by a mine, and Barry's father had hunted for his body parts, like Easter eggs, in the waist-high grass.

The film was nearing its end when the phone rang at ten past nine.

'Barry? Is that the social worker Barry Wheeler?'

'Speaking.'

A pause. Barry could hear a TV, a kettle whistling.

'You look after my mum, Pandora.'

'Of course. Yes. Maria.'

'She talks about me?'

Pandora rarely spoke of Maria. When she did, her head shook and her voice wavered.

'Yes.'

'How is she?'

'Better.' Barry remembered Pandora's interrogating eyes. 'She's had a minor relapse. It happens.'

'I'd like to ask you a favour.'

'Of course.'

'I wonder if you might ask her to make contact with the family lawyer. Once she's better.'

'Regarding what?'

'Regarding her will.'

'Well, she certainly doesn't have testamentary capacity at the moment,' Barry said, his thoughts turning to the property in Richmond.

'I understand that.'

'But I'll pass your message on.'

'Thank you.'

'Once she's well.'

'Much appreciated.'

'Although I'd encourage you to speak to her directly. She is your mother, after all.'

'I'm flying to London in the morning. It's hard to get

time off. From work. And the kids.'

'Of course.'

'Thank you, Barry,' Maria said, and hung up.

Barry sank into the couch and turned up the volume on the TV. He ate the last of his ravioli and watched a bloodied Marlon Brando lamenting the horror.

Pandora was worse. Her euphoria had given way to an angry paranoia.

'Where are my sunglasses?' she yelled when she saw him. 'My diamond-encrusted sunglasses?'

'They should be here somewhere,' Barry said as he watched her rifle through the drawers in her bedside table.

'That's what my mum used to say after she took my old toys to the op shop. *They should be here somewhere!*'

'Pandora.' Barry put a hand on her shoulder. 'Don't stress. We'll find them.'

She sat down on the bed then—appeased, for a moment. She hadn't bothered with make-up today. Her face looked pale, anaemic.

'There was a paper bag when you came in. We put your clothes in it, and the sunglasses too.'

Pandora nodded. She studied her hands, gnarled and knotted like tree roots. 'My daughter's stealing from me.'

Barry felt his stomach leap. 'Why do you say that?'

'Things keep going missing.'

Soon after Barry graduated, a psychiatrist had told him that delusions have their origins in reality. Barry still found it hard, ten years on, to tease the truth from the fantasy.

'We'll find your sunglasses, Pandora. Don't worry.'

Pandora picked at a scab on her wrist. 'There's no one, Barry.'

'I'm here, aren't I?'

'I'm going to die alone.'

It was probably true. Most of Barry's clients died alone. A few lay dead for days before anybody noticed they were gone.

'This is a relapse,' Barry said, hating himself. 'Nobody's dying.'

Barry had only seen his father cry once, at his mother's funeral. That was enough. He sat in the front pew of the church, near the coffin, quietly convulsing. Barry was close enough to see the old man's face. It was as if an epic battle were underway beneath his furrowed brow. Well-meaning hands on shoulders were violently shrugged away. Offers of tissues were met with a dismissive wave of his hand. But every so often a lone tear trickled down his crumpled cheek, and Barry's father hung his head in shame.

The next morning, a Saturday, Barry jumped out of bed with his alarm. The thermostat read five degrees. He made himself a coffee for the journey and drove to Victoria Market through the maze of empty streets. Most people were at home, taking refuge beneath their doonas. Except the doughnut maker. He was there with his van—a glowing, metallic beast in the abandoned car park. A couple of committed patrons paced and rubbed their gloved hands together as they waited. Barry sat on a ledge, nursing what remained of his homemade coffee. As he sipped, his attention turned to a young man with a preschool-aged daughter. He watched the girl's eyes close with delight as she took her first bite of doughnut and then flash wide with fear when her father scolded her for spilling jam on her jumper.

'Next!' the doughnut maker cried, and Barry stood up. There were thirteen residents on his father's floor—twelve now George was gone. Barry ordered a dozen. As he walked to the car, he felt the hot balls of dough warm his palms, like something alive, through the bottom of the paper box.

Allomother

Sunday nights are for planning. I search the internet for the latest exhibitions, concerts and other kid-friendly events. We've been to the main attractions: the museum, the botanical gardens, the children's farm, the gallery. We've sampled babycinos and avocado smash at all but the most pretentious cafes. Sometimes I don't plan anything at all. I plan not to plan—because too much structure can suffocate creativity in a child—and we do silly things like make nappies for Baby from the fallen leaves in my backyard.

Monday nights are for cooking. I bake homemade treats for our outings. Healthy snacks like apricot muesli bars and savoury muffins made with organic pumpkin and goat's cheese. There has to be something to counteract the frozen rubbish that gets dished up at home. *Snap-frozen*, her mother corrects me, but she is just defending the time she spends on the couch watching back-to-back episodes of *House of Cards*.

Tuesday nights are for packing. Or rather checking that my oversized waterproof handbag is adequately stocked. Because when it comes to kids—and Molly in particular—you can never be too prepared. Every so often I get caught out and have to add another item to my list. It's an organic thing, my list, a little like my muesli bars. *Two packets of Dora the Explorer bandaids, one tube of Cancer Council approved nano-free kids' sunscreen, a hat, a cardigan, a spare pair of underwear, a BPA-free water bottle, a lunch box with aforementioned organic snacks, face towels, Molly's second-favourite Barbie doll (Candy, with the blue-biro-coloured hair) and my camera.*

I have one photo. Jules and Mick took everything else—the ultrasound images and DVDs, even the positive pregnancy test I dipped in my urine. It's a selfie taken in the bathroom mirror, with one hand cupping my belly. The phone covers my face. Only my mouth is showing. I'm wearing a grey maternity top from Kmart and a pair of black trackie dacks covered in lint. There are no identifying features. No scars or beauty spots or tattoos of ex-lovers' names. Nothing to prove that it's me. It could be anyone.

*

I'm drinking a watery cappuccino at the zoo cafeteria. Molly is under my chair, feeding discarded chips to a one-legged pigeon. It is three o'clock and the cafe is full. I scan the tables, priding myself on being able to pick the parents from the non-parents. The parents are the ones checking email on their smart phones while their toddler eats marshmallows off the floor. It's the nannas and pops and aunties and uncles who hang, bright-eyed, on every mispronounced word, confident they'll soon be rewarded with a flash of wisdom or comedic genius. Like when Molly compares the mole on my neck to a sultana, or asks me questions I can't answer, like whether fish sleep—and if they do, how do I know, if they never close their eyes?

They took vial after vial of blood. I was terrified, but I needn't have been. My hormone levels were *within normal limits*, and my uterus wasn't *hostile*—who knew organs could be hostile?—like my sister's. It was the proof I had been searching for all these years that I was better than her. But the victory didn't give me the joy I thought it would. I didn't feel like I'd won anything.

'I want to see the ephelants.'

We are in the ape enclosure. A female is nursing her newborn, two young chimps are catapulting from tree to tree, and a large male is lying on the platform-cum-stage, juggling his salmon-pink testicles.

Molly sucks her thumb. She is an elephant person, like her mother. Jules brought me a sandalwood elephant once, as a last-minute gift, at Koh Samui Airport. But that was a long time ago. Back when she and Mick had money to travel. Before IVF, and the miscarriages. Before varicose veins, and Molly.

'Dara's waiting for me,' Molly says.

Dara is the new elephant calf. One of three conceived at the zoo.

'His name means star,' she says, as we turn our back on the chimps. 'Like mine!'

'That's right,' I say, genuinely impressed. 'Yours means star of the sea.'

I don't mention the Hebrew meaning—and the reason Jules and Mick chose it in the end. *Molly. Diminutive of Mary: the wished-for one.*

At strategic points around the zoo there are candy-coloured signs spouting facts about the animals: *Did you know that elephant society has a female-led structure that is often called matriarchal? The oldest female is the matriarch. She determines the group's movements.* I try to explain the words to Molly—to convey the complexity of these awesome beasts—but she just hops on one foot and screams that she needs to wee.

*

I quit my job, which I hated, at the end of the first trimester. In my spare time I drove to faraway suburbs and sat in cafes, chatting to waitresses about what I would name my baby. It was a game. It didn't feel real. It certainly didn't feel dangerous. I was shocked when, at thirty-eight weeks, the doctor told me the baby was breech and I would need a caesarean. I'd never had an operation before.

'You'll be fine,' the anaesthetist said, but I didn't trust him. He was too good-looking to be a doctor.

I watched the painful shrink of Mick and Jules' faces as the orderly pulled me along the corridor. They didn't wave—that would have been too much like farewell. They just stood very still. Only then did I see myself as they did: a vessel for their magic bean. For the first time, clutching each other as if they might drown in the linoleum sea, they looked the part: a mummy and a daddy.

Did you know that the main function of the family unit is the protection of baby elephants? The greater the number of females looking after a calf, the greater its chance of survival.

I looked at Jules and Mick across the expanse of polished oak.

'Just a formality, hon.'

The lawyer was an ageless Chinese woman who could have passed for fourteen or forty. She nudged the thirty-page document towards me.

At birth, the Surrogate will relinquish the Child(ren) to the Biological Father and Biological Mother, and the Biological Father and Biological Mother will assume all parental rights and responsibilities for the Child(ren) from that time forward.

I was twenty weeks pregnant then. She was the length of a banana. Her ears were perfectly formed. I had just started to feel her dart like a slippery fish inside me.

'We wanted to wait,' Jules said, as if reading my mind.

'To make sure it was viable,' Mick explained.

'It?' I snapped and Mick went white. We had found out the sex at the last scan.

'*She.*' Mick corrected himself.

Jules shook her head. The lawyer pulled a pen from her breast pocket. One of those old-fashioned fountain pens with a reservoir and a nib. She placed it at a ceremonious diagonal across the paper.

'I'm not going to steal your child,' I said.

'Of course not,' Jules said, but the baby-faced lawyer disagreed.

'Kids do strange things to people.'

I looked at my sister's stony face and her husband's blotchy, patchwork one. I felt a flutter—the flap of tiny arms, perhaps—below my bellybutton. I picked up the pen.

'They sure do.'

*

154

Dad took me and Jules to the zoo once. I must have been about thirteen. It was a big deal, coming down on the train from Bendigo for the day. We were celebrating Jules getting picked for the under-fifteens hockey team. Mum had to work, but Dad, being a teacher, was off for the school holidays.

I don't think they had elephant calves at the zoo in those days. I don't remember much about the animals, to tell the truth. Mainly I remember how two boys with skateboards stared at Jules on the train. She had just grown breasts— firm things that tented her T-shirt like a couple of smuggled plums—and I remember how she stared out the window, her long, hairless legs neatly tucked beneath her bottom, and how everything in the carriage rattled, it seemed, except for her.

Did you know that baby elephants can have more than one mother? Sometimes a female cow who is not quite ready to have her own baby looks after her younger siblings and cousins. The practice is known as allomothering. The female is the allomother.

It is standing room only at the elephant enclosure. Molly is up on my shoulders. The calf, his eyes red with fright, cowers beneath the belly of an elderly cow. I'm reminded of Nanna's big teak dining table and the long days Jules and I spent playing beneath it. A keeper holds up a loudspeaker. He informs us that an elephant pregnancy lasts nearly two years. There are gasps from the audience. Mothers, mainly. Imagine that, they say, and laugh and rub their deflated bellies.

'You can use this,' Jules said, uncoiling a bandage. 'Or take the drugs.'

My hands crept up towards my breasts. They were hard and lumpy, like pineapples.

'You wrap it tight as you can,' she said, studying the crepe between her fingers. 'Harriet's doula swears by it.'

I took the bandage and retreated to the bedroom. Jules had never asked me to express and I had never offered, even though we both knew it would be the best thing for Molly. I suspect it would have undone her: another thing my body could do that hers couldn't.

It took everything not to scream. Milk seeped through the beige fabric, creating brown stains above my nipples. It hurt like buggery, as my mother would say, but pain was what I wanted. I'd been asleep for the C-section and hadn't been through labour. I needed to feel tissue tearing, the gush of blood, the placenta shearing from the womb. I'd always thought it should be agonising to the point of torture—the final sundering of a child from its mother.

*

In the car on the way home I dissect the day's events.

Did you have fun?

What was your favourite part?

Did you enjoy seeing all the animals?

Molly gives monosyllabic answers and goes back to sucking her dirty thumb. She isn't like me, always looking in the rear-view mirror. She is focused on the road ahead, craning to see what lies around the next bend.

As we park outside her house, Molly sits up straight in her booster seat. Once out, she holds my hand for a millisecond before breaking away to tear off down the driveway. I watch her bang on the front door with two fists and stand on tippy-toes to reach the handle. I can still feel her hot little hand in mine as I see Julie's long silhouette in the doorway. Molly can't get inside fast enough. The house swallows her, hungrily.

White Sparrow

It's hot inside the car. Can't be more than twenty degrees outside, but Bec has been sitting in the Camry for a good half-hour. She'd rather not mix with the other parents, chatting and laughing and asking each other lots of questions.

Ollie will be out soon enough. For a kid who claims to hate school, he takes a long time to leave. But that's Ollie, always trailing behind everybody else. Sometimes Bec forgets. Like during school holidays, when it's just the two of them, and they spend a fortnight pretending the dining table is a pirate ship and the small square of cracked concrete and weeds out the back—their 'inner-city sanctuary'—is a misty Amazonian jungle. And then term starts, and Bec sees the figure of a boy walking towards her, and for whatever reason—the sun is behind him or he is wearing his sports clothes or she is hazy from a bad night's sleep—she doesn't realise that this child, so intent on burying his face in his chest, is, in fact, her Ollie. And then all the fear and the shock come back to roost in her breast, as if they never left.

Bec looks across at the playground. Twins dangle from the monkey bars, their cheeks the colour of beetroot. Beneath the slide, a boy with orange hair shines a magnifying glass at a pile of leaves. A girl in pigtails lies on her stomach in a hanging tyre—arms and legs stretched out, Superman-style—slowly twisting. Bec remembers the way Ollie used to giggle when she pushed him on the swing. He was a brave little bugger back then. Forever falling and sprouting bumps, like hard-boiled eggs, on his forehead.

Tom had never wanted kids—*Who needs all that?* he'd say with a wave of his hand. *Poo and snot and vomit and tantrums and the Wiggles?*—so Bec was nervous when she did the test, but he took it better than she'd expected. Then, while they were watching the footy one day, he'd talked about taking their son to a Bombers game. And then another time, when she was around thirty-eight weeks, she'd caught him in the empty nursery, running his big hands along the edge of the cot.

Finally, on April Fool's Day, Ollie had arrived, and everything changed, but not in the way it should. The midwife said he had *a good pair of lungs on him*, but they all saw it—a big red mark, like a smear of strawberry jam, across his crumpled face. The nurse rubbed Ollie clean with a warm towel, but the mark didn't come off. If anything, it looked redder, angrier. Bec took the child in her arms, but Tom didn't move from the end of the bed. It was only once the baby rooted for his first suckle that Bec finally acknowledged the mark's presence. Tom and the midwife watched as she traced her finger along its wandering edge. For a moment she had them all believing it was a thing of great importance—the coastline of some newly discovered land.

Bec could see it was painful for Tom. On the rare occasions he looked into the cot, he flinched as if someone had struck him. But the worst was when they took Ollie for walks in the pram. Neighbours stopped them in the middle of the street and wanted to take a peek, and though nobody said anything, Bec and Tom both saw it: the sharp intake of breath, the smile that never quite reached their eyes, the pity in their voices as they said, 'Beautiful. Just beautiful.' Those days were the worst. On those days Tom would go to the pub with one of the guys from work. Bec would imagine him, drinking and talking footy and cars until, presumably, he forgot. On those days the resentment was hard to bear. Because Bec knew that no matter what she did, no matter how much she drank, nothing could extinguish this new ache—like a million unrequited first loves—burning inside her chest.

Bec checks her watch. It's late, even for him. She steps out of the car. The lollipop lady, a large woman with cottonwool hair, smiles and leans on her stop sign. A couple of girls with lip gloss and breast buds snigger at something on their iPhones. Bec feels a surge of anxiety. But just as she has composed what she will say to the pinched-looking woman in the office—*My son, Ollie, he's new, the one with a birthmark on his face*—she spots him, walking across the playground with an urgency to his step she hasn't seen for a long time.

His face is shiny with sweat when he reaches the school gates. 'Where's my scroll?'

'No *Hi Mum, had a great day, Mum, thanks for picking me up?*' Bec says, pulling a paper bag from her tote. Ollie snatches the pastry, sticks his nose in its flesh. When they're in the car, Bec turns the air conditioner to full blast. It's not until the third set of lights that either of them speaks again.

'So, really, how was your day?'

She's not sure why she persists, except out of habit. It is Ollie's third week at the school and she knows what the response will be: the universal adolescent reply of a lazy shrug. In this respect her eleven-year-old is well beyond his years. It's still better than the *I don't want to talk about it* that she copped every day at his previous school, so it's a victory, of sorts.

'S'alright,' Ollie spits, through a mouthful of raisins and bread.

Bec is so stunned by his response she doesn't notice the traffic light change to green. The man in the ute behind them shouts and beeps. It is one of those long I'm-going-to-keep-my-hand-on-the-horn-until-you-move type of beeps. Bec jumps to attention, lifts her foot off the brake.

Her next move will be crucial. Lately, raising her son has felt less like parenting and more like taming a wild animal. She feels nostalgic for the days when Ollie was still in kindergarten. Bec didn't appreciate it at the time—she was too busy complaining about the early-morning starts and grubby handprints on the bedroom wall—but now she wishes she could have bottled the love that once poured so freely from those brown eyes. For now she will have to make do with gems like *s'alright*: two individually unremarkable words rolled into the glorious one.

It was never really about the birthmark. But the 'port wine stain', as the doctors called it, provided a focus for their attention—for Bec's concern and Tom's resentment. Tom was not prepared for the witching hours or the poo that looked like mustard or a wife who jumped out of bed to breastfeed but was perennially too tired for sex. As Bec thrived—her cheeks aglow with some new-found zeal—Tom withered. His skin took on that sallow look people get when their kidneys have failed. Only his kidneys were fine.

She practises questions in her mind as she fries pork chipolatas for dinner. *So, what happened today?* Too probing. *Learn anything useful?* Too generic. *You know, in the car, when you said things were all right? What did you mean by that?* Too…clinical psychologist. The five o'clock news provides the much-needed icebreaker.

'Mum!'

She looks up from the foaming fat of the sausages.

'Yes, honey?'

'The sparrow Mr Walton talked about. It's on TV!'

Ollie is sitting cross-legged on the floor, in a rainbow nest of Lego.

'An albino sparrow, one of the rarest birds on earth, has today been spotted in Melbourne's south-western suburbs. Local residents have nicknamed it their "little white angel" and are keeping its exact location secret.'

Ollie has always been obsessed with animals. Not with lions and tigers, like other boys his age, but with insects and birds, rabbits and possums.

'Mr Walton said it's a one in a million sighting.'

'Wow,' Bec says, impressed. Mr Walton is young, with

sleepy eyes and a mop of limp blond hair. Not her type—too feminine—but right now she could kiss him on the lips.

The morning after Ollie's fifth birthday, Tom left. Bec knew it was coming, and in many ways it was a relief. Except for the look in Ollie's eyes when he asked, 'When's Daddy coming back?' and she replied, 'Soon, honey. Very soon.' Because while Tom could barely look his son in the face, Ollie adored his father. He would happily spend three hours on a stool in the corner of the garage watching Tom disassemble the latest broken appliance.

Tom couldn't bear it. 'He's always hanging around. Watching me with his big possum eyes.'

'He wants to be like you,' Bec would say. 'It's normal.'

But that didn't stop the whingeing. Eventually she told Tom to ignore him. Which he did. He snubbed him. He was curt to him. He stayed late at the pub to avoid him. But when Tom got home, Ollie would be waiting, wide-eyed and jumpy, like a puppy. And Bec knew it had to be hard: all that love when he didn't deserve it.

It was a risk, coming to Melbourne. *Better the devil you know*, her mother had always said, and while Ollie had had a tough time in the country, he was surviving. They both were. In the first few months after Tom left, that was enough. But as the years passed and Ollie stopped asking about his dad, Bec thought they could do better. Aim higher. Melbourne seemed as good a place as any. There were enough people that they could disappear, but not so many as to smother them.

They settled in the northern suburbs, in a red brick unit built in the seventies. Bec found a job as a receptionist. She enrolled Ollie in the local school. She dabbled in online dating. Once a week they went to the pool.

Bec puts the plate of sausages, mashed pumpkin and boiled peas on the table.

'Dinner!'

Ollie doesn't need to be called twice. He sits down and plants his fork in the mash.

'So, sparrows, huh?' she says, wiping her hands on her apron before sitting down opposite him.

'Not just a normal sparrow,' Ollie says, shovelling more mash into his mouth. 'A *white* sparrow.'

'I nursed a baby sparrow once. I gave it water with a dropper.'

That lazy shrug again.

'Eat your peas, please.'

Ollie spoons as many peas as he can fit into his mouth. As he chews, bright green pulp spills from the corners of his lips.

'You've got your first treatment tomorrow, remember?'

Ollie swallows. 'With the laser?'

'Yes.'

He forms a gun with his hands, makes a noise, shoots.

When she has finished the dishes, she sits at her desk with her laptop. She types the words *white sparrow* into the Google search bar.

The first hit is a newspaper article. An interview with an ornithologist:

> If there's a funny-looking bird in the nest it almost always gets the flick. Its white colour makes it easy prey. It really stands out.

Bec can't bear to read on. She prints a picture of the bird and snaps her computer lid shut.

She saw Tom, once, after he up and left. He was sitting in a parked car in the street outside Ollie's school. She'd been daydreaming as she waited, thinking about what to cook for dinner, and looking without really looking into the windscreen of a white Corolla. At first all she saw was the reflection of a plane tree, but then, lurking behind the glassy leaves, she found her husband's sheepish face. Bec's heart thumped against her ribs like some kind of caged animal. Then she saw his gaze shift—Ollie, just eight years old, had stepped through the school gates. Looking back, she's not sure what she was afraid of. *He* was the one who'd left *them*. Perhaps he'd had a change of heart. Perhaps it wasn't Ollie who had driven him away at all. Perhaps it had been her all along, with her tuneless singing and unimaginative cooking and endless sanctimonious crap. Perhaps, after three long years, Tom had arrived to reclaim his child. But before Ollie had even got within ten metres of the car, the engine growled back to life and Tom was gone. Again. Ollie was none the wiser, but it left Bec shaken. Literally. Her limbs trembling like the leaves of the plane tree.

Later that night, while Ollie showers, Bec tidies his room. She pulls his lunch box from his schoolbag and puts his dirty clothes in the laundry basket. As she hunts for a soiled sock beneath the bed, something red catches her eye. She pulls it out. A T-shirt. One of Tom's—Bec recognises it straight away. She's not sure how Ollie got his hands on it. Perhaps he'd found it at the back of her wardrobe when they packed up the old house. She sticks her nose in the fabric. It is not Tom she smells, but Ollie. When she hears the bathroom door open, she scrunches the T-shirt up in a ball and shoves it back where she found it. Ollie slinks into the room and climbs into bed. This is Bec's favourite part of the day. Something about the heat of the shower and the flannelette pyjamas softens Ollie, and for five minutes he is her baby again. Bec's thirty-year-old copy of *The Hobbit* lies, splayed, on his bedside table. A collage of photos and stickers and magazine cut-outs hovers above his wet head: ticket stubs from the Lego convention; photos of Nanna's late border collie, Milo; a polaroid of Ollie and Bec, soaked and happy, at the bottom of the river ride at Movie World. And there at the very centre, sticky-taped to the plaster wall, the first-ever photo of the three of them. Bec bleary-eyed and doped up on morphine; Tom perched awkwardly on the edge of the hospital bed; Ollie with what looks like a smile—but is probably gas—on his red face.

Bec pats Ollie's feet through the doona. She pulls a piece of paper from the pocket of her dressing-gown. 'Thought you could add this to your collection.' Ollie studies the black and white picture of the sparrow. They listen to the groans of the water heater. 'You know you don't have to go through with it tomorrow,' Bec says.

'I know.'

'They'll give you something to put on it after. A cream.'

'I know.'

'Not that it's going to hurt.'

'I know, Mum.'

'What was it that the doctor said again? A small sting?'

'Flick of a rubber band.'

Bec kisses Ollie's cheek. In a few years it will be lumpy with pimples. For now, it is hairless and clean. She finds a piece of Blu-Tack on the bedside table and sticks the white sparrow to the bedroom wall. It hangs between a Haigh's chocolate wrapper—Tom's favourite—and a Bombers bumper sticker.

'You know, Ollie, sometimes I think I'm a bit like that white sparrow.'

Ollie nods. 'Mr Walton says there's a white sparrow in everybody.'

Bec tucks the doona up around Ollie's chin. 'I like Mr Walton.'

She switches on the bedside lamp.

'Mum?'

'Yes, honey?'

'Don't worry. About tomorrow.'

'I'm not.' Bec feels a tightness, like the grip of a hand, around her throat. She knows she should say something about Tom—how proud he would be, if he knew. But the words refuse to come.

Ollie picks up his book, wriggles deeper beneath his doona.

'Goodnight, Mum.'

'Goodnight, Ollie. My little man.'

In the muted light of the bedside lamp his birthmark is veiled in shadow. Above his tousled head a paper bird floats like a white angel.

Muse

I've neglected her.

Her ceilings are soft with cobwebs. Her garden is choked
with weeds. Her fence leans, like buckteeth, out onto the
footpath. She is getting old, and noisy. Like me, with my
snorts and grunts and farts that catch even me by surprise.
Her doors creak, her heating claps itself to life, and her pipes
splutter up their rusty sputum.

I used to wander from room to room, hunting for
memories. The ladder of lines marking Bea's height behind
her bedroom door. The sun-bleached armchair where Lola
nursed Bea day and night for months on end. I wanted to
bathe in nostalgia—I never expected to find something new.
But there they were, a pair of lace undies at the bottom of

the rosewood chest. The Lola I knew only ever wore ankle-length skirts and chunky orthopaedic sandals. The discovery unnerved me. Had I been the one to go first, I would have left no mysteries behind. Lola would have known my clothes better than me. She would have seen the shadows of stains long gone, and they still would have bothered her.

It is autumn. The Japanese maple is shedding its apricot leaves. I pick a book from the shelf in the lounge room, but hard as I try, I can't read tonight. I'm relieved when the phone rings—the urgent cry of the old mobile Bea insists I carry around with me. Only Bea, and a few telemarketers, ever call me on it.

'Hello?'

'Dad.'

'Bea.'

This is how we talk. We acknowledge each other's existence, nothing more.

'I'm coming over.'

'What if I have company?'

She sighs. 'Do you?'

'Not tonight.'

'Good. I mean, not *good*.' She clears her throat. 'You know what I mean.'

I hear voices, a siren, somebody's phone.

'Where are you?'

'On a tram.' She is already losing patience with me. 'And Dad?'

'Yes?'

'I'm bringing Edwina.'

'Of course.'

'So don't say anything stupid.'

Bea likes to have the last word, and she usually makes it bite.

I sweep away the crumbs between the toaster and the kettle. I spray the stovetop with Windex and wipe it down with a sponge. It is a superficial clean—just enough to stop Bea from worrying. Lola, with her tenacious broom, always kept the insects at bay, but now the ants trace invisible maps across the floorboards, collecting breadcrumbs as they go. The spiders follow, emerging from the heating vents to knit sticky webs in secret corners. One day, I think, someone will find me, tangled in the bougainvillea, with centipedes crawling out of my eyes.

Bea arrives at seven, on the dot. When I open the door she pushes past—blaming her bad manners on the bags of hot food in her hands. I look at the girl left behind on the doorstep. She is a pretty thing, fresh-faced, with pale skin. I decide to like her.

'I'm Evan,' I say, extending an arm.

The girl takes my hand as if to shake it and then pulls me into an embrace. She leaves a star of wet saliva on my cheek.

'It's so great to meet you. Finally,' she says.

We follow Bea into the kitchen, where she is searching frantically through the drawers.

'Where have you put the placemats, Dad?'

'I don't know.' I am still feeling the wetness on my cheek and trying not to imagine this long-limbed girl in bed with my daughter. I suppress an image of them sleeping late on a Sunday morning, naked among crumpled sheets.

'Honestly, Dad, do you ever put things back where you find them?'

'The table can get stained for all I care,' I say, and smile sideways at a visibly awkward Edwina.

'Mum would've wanted us to use the placemats.'

Here we go. Is this how it's always going to be? The two of us scrambling for Lola's approval? Even when she's dead?

Bea finds the precious placemats and we bury our heads in the food. Rice is piled onto plates and thick green curry is spooned on top.

'So. Edwina. What do you do?' I say, and my daughter flashes me a look.

'Ed's an artist.'

'Can't Edwina speak for herself?'

'I don't mind,' Edwina says. 'But I'm hardly an artist.'

'Of course you are!' Bea turns to me. 'She was highly commended in the Archibald.'

I nod, pretending to know what the Archibald is—presumably a prize, an accolade of sorts.

'Bea tells me you're a bit of a painter yourself,' Edwina says between mouthfuls.

'I played with a few oils, when I was young. But I haven't been near a brush in years.'

'You should really get back into it,' Bea says, and now I am the one shooting looks. Edwina, naturally more intuitive, or kind, sees my discomfort and changes the subject.

We all relax a little once the wine has coated our insides. I make a fire and put Billie Holiday on the stereo.

'Not this shit again,' Bea says, but as I move to change it Edwina grabs my arm.

'Leave it,' she says. 'I like it.'

She's too nice, I think. Bea will chew her up and spit her out when she's done.

'I'm going for a smoke,' Bea says, and when she leaves I feel relieved and then guilty for feeling relieved.

'I'd love to see your paintings one day,' Edwina says once we are alone. She cups her steaming mug of tea with two hands. 'Bea says you're very talented.'

I offer Edwina a Tim Tam. 'I might have a couple of things in the shed. Maybe next time you come over.'

'I'd like that.' Edwina smiles. The song on the CD finishes, leaving us with the pop and crackle of burning wood. I poke one of the logs. It sizzles some more.

'I don't know if you're interested,' Edwina begins, 'but I do a life drawing class once a week on Smith Street. We're always looking for new people to join.'

Before I have time to answer, Bea is back in the room, holding Shakespeare, our Persian cat, in her arms.

'It's fucking cold,' she says, collapsing into the couch and burying her nose in Edwina's hair. I feel my cheeks burn with embarrassment. Or jealousy. Or both.

'We should probably get going.'

'Of course.'

'Thanks for the tea.'

'And the wine.'

We hug and Edwina leaves a matching kiss on my other cheek. 'No pressure,' she whispers as she stuffs a piece of paper inside my pocket.

I watch their car disappear down Sydney Road before I pull out her parting gift. It is a flyer, with a sketch of a female nude in the background.

MARCEL'S STUDIO

UNTUTORED LIFE DRAWING CLASSES

TUESDAY NIGHTS 6.30–8.30

$20 PER CLASS

ALL WELCOME

*

Her name was Ana. She owned the milk bar at the end of our street. There was a room at the back of her shop, and that's where we did it. Even now, I feel a swell in my boxers at the sound of a cash register rattling closed.

When news of the affair finally came out, everybody was shocked. Lola was beautiful. She didn't know it—she pulled her hair into a severe ponytail and covered her pointy breasts with shapeless cardigans—but to everybody else it was clear. She had smooth skin, translucent like a half-cooked egg, and big, blue-grey eyes. Ana, on the other hand, was not beautiful. Her breasts sagged over the soft rolls of her belly, and when she wore a tight top (which was most days), big sweat marks, like bruises, bloomed in her armpits. I didn't love her, but she was real. She didn't slip out of my hands like silk when I held her.

I wake up with a headache. I look at the clock: ten am. Shakespeare is clawing at my feet. I roll out of the warm nest of sheets and lean down to stroke him. In the kitchen there are Tim Tam crumbs under the stools and dirty mugs on the benchtop. I catch sight of Edwina's crumpled flyer on the floor and pick it up. I've never done life drawing before. I wonder how it works. Does the model strip down in front of the class? Or does she appear in a satin robe, which she lets drop at the ring of a bell? I look at the sketch again, focusing now on the underbelly of the breast. I imagine how lovely it would be to recreate that gentle upward slope of flesh and then the sudden sting of nipple.

I go for a walk. I follow the trail of clouds created by my breath. They lead me here. Every path leads me here. To the milk bar. The Chinese man who now owns it is sweeping leaves from the footpath. I feel an urgent need for Ana, electrifying Ana, with her strong thighs and brassy laugh.

I am alone. Maybe it's been cancelled. Maybe it was a joke. Maybe Bea and her lover are hiding behind a wheelie bin laughing at me. But just as I'm about to leave, Edwina arrives.

'Evan!' she says, kissing me again. 'I'm so glad you could make it.'

'Yeah,' I say, schoolboy shy.

'You'll love it. I promise.'

We climb a groaning staircase and emerge, breathless, into a light-filled space. On the floor a small radiator burns near a pile of patchwork pillows. Edwina gets to work, assembling her easel and lining up her broken sticks of charcoal. She beams at me.

'I'm right,' I say, holding up my sketchpad.

People filter in. An Asian man sits on a milk crate and sharpens his pencils with a rusty knife. Others gather around the kettle, making tea and helping themselves to mugs of red wine from a cask. Fearful of conversation, I wander over to the window. A tram rattles by and a couple of rugged-up passengers step out. They cover their wet noses with their scarves. I think of home and it feels like a wretched place—a playground for insects and ghosts.

I'm still staring out the window when the session begins. All matters practical are dealt with while my back is turned: the disrobing, the arrangement of pillows, the adjustment of the light. By the time I turn around the stage has been set. In the centre of the room, bathed in light, a white beauty.

As long as I can remember, I've preferred the company of women. This may be because the important men in my life were all bastards. My father admired two things: brutality and stoicism. I never saw him cry—not when he shot our dog, or beat my mother, or lost his thumb to a machine at work. For a long time he was the toughest, coldest man I knew. And then I met Lola's dad. Back in those days there were few people in Melbourne who hadn't heard of Professor Duvall. The week before our introduction, he'd drilled a big hole through the police commissioner's skull, and—as he liked to point out repeatedly—saved the dirty bugger's life.

Professor Duvall arranged our first meeting at the hospital. Lola was nervous. I could tell by the way she played with the edge of her scarf. He finally appeared, half an hour late, on a cloud of white-coated underlings. He didn't say hello but threw me the keys to his Peugeot 404 and ordered me to drive him home. It was a good-looking car, sleek black lines, tan leather interior—I should have been proud to be at the wheel of such an impressive beast. But it was impossible not to see this charade for what it was. A test.

She didn't exactly purr in my hands, but I got the three of us back to Hawthorn in one piece. Surprisingly, the professor didn't take much notice of my driving along the way. He and Lola chatted happily in the back seat, and only once did he lean forward to say, 'Nothing quite like French engineering!'

Dinner went off without a hitch. I didn't spill anything, and I used my utensils from the outside in, just as Lola had instructed me to. I laughed at the professor's jokes. I drank, I relaxed. By the time Lola excused herself from the table to help her mother with dessert, my guard was down.

'Cautious, eh?' he asked, once the women were out of earshot.

'Sorry?'

'A cautious driver.'

'Nothing wrong with being cautious,' I said. The wine had given me confidence.

'When you've got another man's life in your hands, you've got to think fast, take risks. You can't afford to be *cautious*.'

'I—'

'You know the difference between you and me, son?'

I gripped the edge of my chair.

'I have the whole world on my plate, and you'll never even get a taste.'

At that moment the women returned to dispense sweet chocolate tarts with even sweeter smiles.

'*Bon appétit!*' the professor cheered, slapping his wife playfully across her aproned rump.

The model has short hair and a plain but pleasant face. I wouldn't look twice at her if she walked past me on the street, but on the page she's lovely, with creamy skin and the limbs of a ballerina.

'Wow,' a voice says. It's Edwina.

'How'd you go?' I ask, ignoring her little exclamation and adding some last-minute shading to the fingers. 'I can't seem to get the hands quite right.'

'Shut up.'

I stop drawing.

'You know it's good,' she says, and though she is smiling there is a bite to her words. 'Just take the compliment.'

'Okay,' I say. 'Thanks.'

'You're even better than I expected.'

Lola would never get naked in front of me. If I happened to walk into the bathroom after she'd just had a shower I might catch a glimpse of a breast, but only for a second, until the towel was secured firmly in place. Sex was something we did with the lights off, fumbling under the covers, finding the pieces and fitting them together in the dark. Towards the end, we didn't even do that.

*

Edwina and I are standing outside in the cold when she finally comes down the stairs. She stops at the bottom and shakes out a cigarette. Someone offers her a light. She looks different in clothes—less magical—but she's still a celebrity in this place.

'Who's the new guy?' she says, without addressing anyone in particular. I'm grateful when Edwina speaks up.

'That's Evan. My friend.'

'Nice to meet you, Evan,' the model says and offers me a limp hand. 'Daniella.' She barely looks at me before flicking her cigarette to the ground. 'Gotta go. My ride's here.'

A man on a black motorbike stops in front of the studio. Daniella puts her helmet on and climbs on the back. There is a puff of diesel and leather and smoke.

'That's not her real name,' Edwina whispers as they disappear behind a tram.

I hang my best sketch on the wall. She has her back to me. A swell of buttocks narrows, in a gentle curve, to a tiny waist. Her backbone climbs—a string of pearls—to that craning neck and teasing glimpse of face. I have her here, caught in a sketch. Daniella.

The mobile vibrates on the bedside table and Bea's name appears on the screen. The ring and flashing letters are insistent, but I can't face her tonight. She's angry and itching for a fight. Edwina is our new Lola and she doesn't want to share.

I've never liked doctors. But I despised them after I got married. It wasn't just that every doctor I met seemed to know and worship Professor Duvall. It was more than that. He had sown the seed of a delusion in my brain (which was, granted, fertile ground for such things) that the entire medical fraternity was looking down on me.

I dread my visits to Dr Jayawickrama. He doesn't deserve this. Lola adored him. Toward the end of her illness, he even made a few house calls—like a village doctor, complete with his bag of potions. But I can't help it. For me, he will always be the man who diagnosed my wife with cancer.

As I step inside the consulting room, I see the bed where Dr Jay used to examine Lola. My knees tremble—I'm relieved when he offers me a seat.

'Your cholesterol results are a lot worse, Evan,' he says, turning from the computer screen to me. 'Are you taking care of yourself?'

'Doing my best.'

'I'm concerned about you,' he says, his brow furrowed. 'It's been five years since Lola passed. And you look dreadful.'

'Are doctors allowed to say that to their patients?'

'We've known each other a long time. We're friends.'

I'm not so sure, I think. I look at the family photo on the

doctor's desk, but the people in the snapshot are strangers. Lola probably knew their names, probably sent them a handmade card at Christmas. He is confusing me with her.

'If you want to talk...' he goes on.

'Thanks, doc. But I'll be right.'

And even the good doctor Jayawickrama knows when to give up a fight.

I never asked Lola's father for her hand. I choked. But Lola never knew. Nobody knew. Except me. And the professor.

I had every intention of asking him. We were in the drawing room (I had never known people to have drawing rooms before) and he had offered me a glass of port.

'How's work?'

'Not bad.'

'Hardly life and death, is it?' he said and passed me his cigar.

'It's money. For some people that's more important than life and death.' I puffed on the cigar, which triggered a paroxysm of coughing.

'Can't handle the good life, eh?' he said and slapped me hard across the shoulder. 'That will have to change if you're planning on staying with my daughter.'

'That's actually what I wanted to talk to you about,' I said, taking a large swig of port for extra courage. 'Sir.'

'Really,' he said, and then, before I could respond, he

added, 'Because if you want my blessing, you can forget it.'

I opened my mouth to speak, but no words would come. Instead, my stomach purged hot fluid through my lips and onto the fine Persian rug.

Daniella. She's crept inside my brain and her languid legs are dangling before my eyes. As I stare at my sketch on the wall, its imperfections taunt me. Soon all I can see are the faults. Her arms are too long. Her head is too small. I can't take it anymore. I tear it down.

Bea finds me in the living room with the torn paper in my hands. I don't know how long I've been sitting here. It might have been an hour, or half a day.

'Why didn't you tell me?' she asks.

But I'm not in the mood for her questions. 'I didn't realise I needed your permission.'

'For fuck's sake.' She stands up to light a cigarette.

'You know you can't smoke in here.'

'I can do whatever the fuck I like.'

'Your mum wouldn't like it,' I say, and regret the words as soon as they've left my mouth.

Our eyes lock. 'Mum's dead,' Bea says. 'Do you get that, Dad?'

'You think I, of all people, don't know that? What the hell's wrong with you?'

'What's wrong with me?' she snaps. 'What's wrong with

me is that I've lost my mother and I can't even talk to my father about it.' She throws her hands in the air.

'What do you want to talk about?' I say, gentler now.

The tears are falling hard and fast.

'Forget it,' she says. 'I don't even know why I bother.'

'I'm sorry I didn't tell you about the class.'

'Just forget it.' She scoops Shakespeare up from the floor. He purrs. He's always loved Bea. 'There are some groceries in the kitchen. I bumped into Dr Jay on the weekend and he said you could do with some good food.'

This time I see it as it happens. She arrives in a cognac-coloured leather jacket and frayed blue jeans. Marcel greets her at the door and ushers her into the bathroom on the second floor, where there are charcoal handprints across the walls. We stop our chatter and take our positions, either at our easels or perched upon our favourite milk crates. When she finally removes her robe, she doesn't throw it back like a cape, but steps out of it, slowly, covering the sprinkling of hair between her legs until the last minute.

I know her curves now. I have a sense of her in my mind. This time I see different things, hidden things. Like the ladder of red lines along her forearm—it takes me a while to recognise them for what they are.

Edwina isn't here, and during the break I wander over to the window. I look out at the street below. An old man weaves through the traffic with a half-empty beer bottle in his hand. But I'm not really watching him. I'm wishing her to me. I am pleading with the universe to bring her to me. And it works.

'You're getting better,' Daniella says.

'Thank you,' I reply. 'I'm getting to know you, I guess.'

'Are you?' she says, hugging her robe around her and cupping a mug of coffee to her lips. She looks me straight in the eye.

'No. I mean, I don't know.'

My nervousness pleases her. 'You certainly noticed my battle scars.' She lifts the sleeve of her robe and points to the scarlet marks on her arm.

'They're part of you. Your story,' I say, and cringe at my own sentimentality.

She cocks her head to the side. 'It's not as romantic as you make it sound.'

The bell on the alarm clock rings. Our time is up.

Nobody is waiting for me. Nobody will notice if I'm late getting home. Except a cat. And even he will find someone else to feed him. Her black knight isn't here tonight. He hasn't arrived on his gleaming black beast. I'll just make sure she's safe, I tell myself. There's no harm in it.

Daniella is the last one to leave. Marcel kisses her goodbye at the door. Two kisses, European style. She starts walking.

She moves at a leisurely pace, stopping to look at a polka-dot dress and fix her hair in a shop window reflection. I hang back, unnoticed—an old man with a scarf wrapped around his ears, invisible to everyone. At the intersection she stops, places a cigarette between her lips and uses both hands to shelter the flame from a sudden blustering wind. She takes a long, slow drag, shutting her eyes and relishing the smoke as it warms her from the inside out. A car drives past and a man leans out.

'Come home with me!' he yells.

'Fuck off!' she yells back.

It is a wintry Tuesday night, and apart from a few smokers outside restaurants and pubs, the streets are empty. Daniella's boots tap on the concrete. The street she lives on is a quiet one, dimly lit. Her single-fronted terrace is shrouded in trees and shadows. The boyfriend must be out, I think. I see her walk up to the front door in the darkness. And then she's gone. Consumed by the big black house.

Bea insists on seeing my sketches. I shouldn't be nervous, but I am. She stands back and squints before leaning in needlessly close. She moves as if to speak and then, at the last moment, stops herself. I can't bear it.

'So?'

She turns to face me. 'You're better than I remember.'

'Really?' Her words give me more pleasure than I could have anticipated.

'Mum would be so proud.'

But now she's ruined it. I think back to last night. Daniella's house.

'What do you like about it?' I say, to change the subject. She could cut me down, but she doesn't.

'I like the fluidity of the lines. I like your sensitivity to your subject.'

This is as close to a moment as we'll get. I put my hand on her shoulder. 'Thank you, Bea.'

'This drawing stuff is good for you. Therapeutic.' She picks up her bag. She's always in such a hurry—to do things, to get away from me. 'Have you been back to see Dr Jay?'

'Not yet.'

'Such a nice man. Maybe you should pay him a visit.'

But I give her the same answer I gave him.

'I'll be right.'

Nostalgia distorts things. Like this photo I'm looking at now. It's of Bea, sitting on a plastic unicorn in some park. Lola is standing behind her and they're both smiling at the camera. It's summer, and Lola is wearing a sunflower dress. It seems so perfect, I'm almost tempted to wish myself back there. But minutes after the photo was taken, Bea fell off the unicorn and knocked out a tooth on the way down. I don't want to relive that. I don't want to remember Bea's howls and her mother's bloodied hands as we sped down Sydney Road to the hospital.

This is how I spend my time, now that I'm old. I stare at things—photos, paintings, trinkets—and I reminisce. When I was younger, I used to wonder what old people did once they retired. I'd imagine them playing a round of golf or having marathon coffee sessions with their friends—anything that was better than going back to my windowless office after lunch. But now I'm here, and it's not the luxury I thought it would be.

I wake up early. As I've gotten older, I've found it harder and harder to sleep in. If I had one wish, I'd wish for the sleep of a teenager—a deep and restful nothingness lasting ten or twelve hours. As it is, I wake up at least twice a night just to go to the toilet. When I do, it takes me a lifetime to get the damn thing going, and then another lifetime to make it stop.

In the mornings I make myself an instant coffee and a piece of toast. I feed Shakespeare. Later on I go to the milk bar to get some milk, or to buy the *Herald Sun*. In the afternoons I check the mail, and then sometimes, in the summer months, I watch a bit of cricket. Every day I pray for some variety, and then, when my prayers are answered, I'm seized with anxiety.

Now I have an aim, a goal to set my sights upon. Tuesdays. My life is a countdown to Tuesdays. Even the remaining days seem less banal. On those days I visit art shops. Art shops, I've found, are wonderful places. The shop assistants let me spend a good part of the day in there, exploring the shelves, trying pens out on the tiny stacks of paper provided for that very purpose. There are blank canvases stacked like fallen dominoes against the walls, and brushes with fine, silky hairs. There are thick tubes of paint with evocative names like 'midnight blue' and 'fire-engine red' and 'grass green' and 'mars black'.

On this particular day I pick out a box of charcoal sticks and take them to the register.

'That'll be seven dollars eighty, thanks.'

I hand over a ten-dollar note.

The girl picks change from the mouth of the register. 'You an artist?' she asks.

'Yes. Sort of. Not really.'

She smiles and hands me my change.

I'm riding high as I walk down Smith Street to the studio. I have my green Coles bag on my shoulder, and in it my sketchpad and new tools. I walk past the hipsters sipping their organic beer. I'm an artist, I think, and even they can see it.

I bound up the stairs. Marcel says, 'Hello, Evan,' and I'm flattered that he remembers my name. He mustn't remember everyone, I think to myself—only the good ones. I take up my regular spot near the window and look around the room. The Asian man is here again. I spot Edwina chatting by the urn to some guy with a nose-ring. She waves, and I wave back. There's only one newcomer tonight. I can tell he's new from the way he's sitting. He's unsure of himself, with no way of gauging how talented he is compared to the rest of us. He gives me confidence. I pour myself a generous mug of red wine.

Marcel enters the room with a smile on his face. 'Good evening, everyone,' he says in a loud voice. 'I'd like to introduce you all to our new model.'

New model. I don't hear much else after that. She's much older than Daniella, and voluptuous, with a head of wild grey hair. Edwina smiles at me. She's excited.

Marcel goes on. 'Peggy's a very experienced model. And so very beautiful, no?'

Peggy doesn't waste any time. She immediately drops her gown and starts posing for the one-minute warm-ups. My confidence crumbles. The charcoal feels strange between my fingers—heavy and foreign. I rip out page after page, and the staccato noise of the paper tearing from the ring-bound spine attracts attention from others in the class.

I can't do it. The lighting is off. Her head is too big for her body. Her pose is stiff and unreal. My neck heats up under my collar. I feel ten pairs of eyes on me as I pack up my things and make a clumsy exit.

Outside, the cold air is a relief. Lola used to talk about that feeling of not being able to breathe, but I've never understood it until now. A panic attack. That was Dr Jay's diagnosis when Lola described the sensation to him.

'Everything okay?'

Marcel has followed me out.

'Yes,' I say. I need to come up with some explanation for my erratic behaviour. 'I felt sick. All of a sudden.'

'It can get a little hot up there sometimes,' he says, pulling a packet of cigarettes from his pocket. 'Smoke?'

I shake my head.

'Good for you.' He lights his cigarette, inhales. Smoke billows from his nose. 'She's a great model, no?'

'Daniella?'

He looks at me quizzically.

'No. Peggy.'

'Yes. Of course.' I nod. 'She's great. I'm just not in the zone tonight.'

Marcel puts a hand on my shoulder. 'It happens.'

Weeks pass. I stop eating. I stop sleeping. Bea starts dropping by. She makes excuses each time she comes: she's in the area; she's found an old DVD I might like. But I can see the concern in her eyes. I can see what's happening too. My face is becoming pale and wan beneath its growing beard. I'm starting to smell. My bones are jutting out as if trying to escape through my papery skin.

I can't believe it when it happens. In the five years since Lola's been gone, it's never happened before. I expect Bea to be angry, but she isn't. Just goes to show how worried she must be. Lola's birthday. The one day of the year when Bea and I agree to put our weapons down. And this year I've forgotten it.

We usually pack a light lunch (with a few of Lola's favourites, like blue brie and teacake) and drive down the Great Ocean Road to the exact spot—the fifth lookout point—where we scattered her ashes. Lola was born in Nice, in the south of France, and she loved the water.

Thank God for Bea. She's taken care of everything. The car is full of fuel and there's a basket of bread and fruit in the boot. All I had to do was get dressed. We find a sheltered place to set down our towels, and then, between mouthfuls of rich cheese and gulps of cheap red wine, we take turns reading Lola's favourite poems. Today, Bea reads 'The Open Sea' by Dorothea Mackellar. She takes her time, savouring the words, waiting for them to catch the breeze and fly far out to sea.

'Beautiful,' I say. I mean it.

'I thought it was a good choice for today.'

Why can't it always be like this? I look into the foaming mouth of the ocean. It's late June and there's a chill in the air. I stand up. 'I'm going for a swim.'

'Don't be ridiculous,' Bea says, licking dip from her fingers and lying back on her towel. She thinks I'm joking, but I'm not. I'm overwhelmed by a sudden urge to go in the water. 'Dad!' she shouts as I run down the beach, shedding layers of clothing as I go. I'm not wearing bathers and I run into the icy water in only my boxers. It's like a hard slap in the face, and it feels good. The sky overhead is grey and there are a few heavy clouds foretelling rain. A lone seagull circles above me, searching the choppy blue expanse for food. I'm waking up.

Her house looks different during the day. It's one of those single-fronted terraces with a corrugated roof. From the street you can see a red lamp in the corner of the window, and a bookcase, bursting with books, next to the mantelpiece. I haven't seen it from the inside, but I imagine a respectable amount of mess—dirty coffee mugs, discarded scarves and mismatched socks strewn across her bedroom—and maybe even a few kitsch collectables like a lava lamp or a glazed clay ashtray in the living room.

I've learnt a lot about Daniella these past few weeks. She doesn't have a fixed schedule. Some days she doesn't go out at all. Other days she's up early and leaves the house with wet hair and a piece of buttered toast in her hand. She always sits on the left side of the tram, and on Wednesday mornings she does a pilates class at the YMCA. It's rather amazing she hasn't noticed me—just goes to show how invisible I've become.

Tonight she's looking at DVDs at the local video store. A pimply teen is shovelling microwave popcorn into his mouth as he watches the newest release on a television mounted above the door. I read his name tag: *Jackson, Assistant Manager.* I'm completely lost in this place. Bea brings me DVDs every once in a while, but I hardly ever get around to watching them. Just the machine puts me off. It always starts flashing instructions when I try to use it. *Set time. Eject. Power off.* Daniella knows what she wants, though. She's already at the counter, waiting for the assistant manager to take time out from his movie and popcorn to serve her. I decide to make a move. I grab the first DVD I see on the weekly hire shelf and line up behind her.

Daniella smiles at me over her shoulder. I smile back. She passes the DVD case across the desk to Jackson, and when he turns to fetch the disc, she speaks to me.

'Do I know you from somewhere?'

'I was just about to say the same thing.'

'Your face looks really familiar.'

'And yours.' I pretend to stumble upon a misplaced memory. 'Did you ever do a life drawing class?'

She blushes ever so faintly.

'Are you an artist too?' I say, and look away. I've never been a good liar.

'Actually I was the model.'

'Ah, yes. Now I remember.'

'But that was months ago. I don't model anymore.'

'Really? From what I remember, you were very good. Very...' I search for an appropriate word. 'Professional.'

Jackson is happy to let us chat. He sits back down and crams another handful of popcorn into his mouth.

'Thanks,' Daniella says. 'But I had some issues with the guy who ran the class.'

'Marcel?'

'Yeah, just money stuff,' she says and pushes a ten-dollar note across the counter.

'Due back by seven pm tomorrow,' Jackson says, turning up the volume on the television.

'Well, it was good to see you.' Daniella picks up her DVD. She is slipping away from me again.

'You too.'

The bell on the door jingles as it closes, and for the first time I look at the DVD I picked off the shelf. Aliens and scantily clad women dominate the cover. 'Think I'll give this one a miss,' I say, and put the movie back where I found it. Jackson merely shrugs.

I wonder if there's time to catch her. I scan the street outside and am relieved when I spot her red beanie bobbing up and down near the intersection. I move so fast that by the time I reach her I can hardly speak.

'What's the matter?' she asks. 'Did I leave my wallet behind?' She fumbles in her oversized handbag. 'I'm forever doing shit like that.'

'No—' I catch my breath. 'I just wanted to ask you something.'

'Oh?' she says, and I'm pleased to see curiosity creep into her face.

'You see, I've been having my own problems with Marcel and the drawing class.'

Daniella raises her eyebrows.

'But I miss drawing. And you were such a good model— from what I remember at least—that I was wondering...well, I was wondering if you'd be interested in modelling for me.'

She doesn't say anything at first.

'I'd pay you well, of course,' I add.

She looks me up and down, as if appraising how much I can afford. 'How well?'

I'm disappointed by her businesslike tone.

'Fifty dollars an hour.'

She hardly hesitates. 'Okay. It's a deal.'

I'm dumbfounded.

'So I guess I should probably introduce myself,' she says and hangs a cigarette from the corner of her mouth. 'Seems only fitting before I get naked in front of you again.' She puts the cigarette packet back in her bag and holds out a gloved hand. 'Daniella.'

'Oh yes, of course. And I'm Evan,' I reply.

'Evan.' She thinks for a moment. 'Yes, I do remember you.'

When I return home, I see the house through Daniella's eyes. I start at the old man smell as I walk through the front door, cringe at the cat hair smeared across the curtains, and the coffee mugs with furry rims. I can't possibly bring her here. I spend the next week cleaning. I fill the regular bin, the recycling bin and even the green wheelie bin with rubbish. It feels good.

I thought Lola's last surprise for me was the pair of lace undies in the rosewood chest. But all this time, the big one has been sitting behind a leg of the desk in the master bedroom. Our bedroom. It wasn't like Lola to be careless, especially not with something of such consequence. It makes me think she wanted me to find it.

3.30 at Merri Creek, our spot. A few words scribbled on the back of a receipt. The note is many years old, but the immediacy of the words makes me picture some mystery man still waiting for Lola down on the banks of the creek. I imagine him to be tall and distinguished—because surely that's what Lola would have been looking for, something different from me—but when I try to envisage his face, I draw a blank. I wonder if he made her happy. I wonder if he made her scream. I should feel vindicated, but I don't. Ana and I never wrote little love notes to each other. We never had a 'spot'. Lola even did affairs better than me.

I'm tempted to tell Bea. She wouldn't believe it at first— not her precious perfect mother—but then I'd show her the note and even she wouldn't think me capable of making up such a story. But I know what would happen. She would make excuses. She would say that Lola was lonely, that the marriage was already over. She would look at me like she did on the day she found me with Ana, all those years ago— with hurt, disappointment and disgust like black clouds across the green of her eyes. I can't compete with a ghost. I've tried before, and the ghost always wins.

The day Bea found me with Ana was the worst day of my life. Lola was doing casual teaching at the local primary school and her hours were predictable. Ana had wanted to close the shop for the afternoon and I'd invited her back home. Bea wasn't meant to finish school until three, but—as I found out months later—she had come down with a migraine (her first and last) and had been sent home by the school nurse. To this day, I live in hope that the migraine clouded what she saw when she walked into that room. I have played it out over and over in my head. Did she see my bare arse or Ana's swinging breasts? Did she recognise the hunger in the way the clothes were strewn wildly across the room?

Whatever she saw, it was enough to make her scream—
a haunting, high-pitched scream that still disturbs my
dreams. And then she fled. I looked at Ana, pulled on a pair
of pants and followed at breakneck speed, nearly slipping on
her abandoned stockings as I careered down the hall, but Bea
had barricaded herself in her room.

'Bea…' I pleaded at her door. 'It's not what it looked like.'

'Do you think I'm a fucking idiot?' she shouted, her voice
wet with tears.

'Of course not.'

'I'm telling Mum.'

Of course you are.

'Can we talk?' I asked. I felt her weight lighten against
the door. As it gave way, she dived onto the bed and buried
her face in a pillow. I kneeled on the floor beside her. 'Bea,
I don't really know what to say.'

'You're disgusting.'

I moved to the edge of the bed. 'I still love your mum.'

'You're disgusting!' She threw her pillow on the floor
and sat up. I felt her fists beating against my chest. 'You're
disgusting!' she said again. And she wouldn't stop. She just
kept saying it—'You're disgusting!'—until I couldn't take
it anymore. I wanted it to stop. I wanted her to stop. So
I pushed her off me. I can still see the shock in her eyes as
her head hit the cupboard door. And then the blood came.
I remember the blood. There was so much blood.

At the hospital, Bea talked to the doctor in the emergency room by herself. I could only hear muffled voices from where I sat outside. I wondered what she was saying. Was she telling them her story? At any moment I expected some stern representative from the Department of Human Services, or even the police, to come and take me away—to punish me for being a bad husband and father, for almost killing my teenage daughter. But the doctor was smiling when he eventually re-emerged.

'She's going to be fine,' he said. 'Just three stitches that will need to come out in a week.' I looked hard, but I couldn't see any revulsion in his eyes—at least nothing beyond what I was accustomed to. And then, as he was about to leave, he stopped. 'Is it true?'

'Is what true?' My heart was racing. Yes, it was true: I was an adulterer and a child abuser, and he should do his duty and report me to the authorities.

'Was Professor Duvall really your father-in-law?'

The affair was the scandal of the year on our street. An Aussie cheating on the daughter of a prominent neurosurgeon with the fat Croatian woman from the milk bar. In those days gossip didn't get much more titillating than that. But that was when people still took the time to get to know their neighbours—when they would wave instead of nervously eyeing each other from the safety of their front lawns. So it wasn't long before anyone and everyone knew. It was a strange and embarrassing thing, to talk to Lola about it. At least I only ever had to live through it once. After that day she never mentioned it again.

'So, did you get it out of your system?' she said. Her tone wasn't angry—more matter of fact. 'Because if you didn't, we'll have to get a divorce, but if you did, I'm willing to forgive you.' That's how she was: clinical and practical, like her father.

Lola's father hadn't lived long enough to celebrate my downfall. He was killed by a haemorrhage so large only someone of his skill could have drained it. (God knows his registrar gave it a good go, but the professor did nothing by halves and his death was no exception.) In some ways, I would have preferred it if he had still been alive at the time—I could have tolerated the lectures, the awkwardness, the smug looks, the *I told you so's*. Anything but his ghost, taken up residence in his daughter's eyes.

We never made love again after that. I never made love again. It was my punishment.

I last saw Ana in the fruit and veg shop at Barkly Square. She looked old under the fluorescent lights. Her doughy cheeks sagged, and she had the shadow of a moustache above her lips.

'Ana.'

It took some time for her to recognise me.

'Evan,' she finally said, with that ever-so-slight European accent she had. 'I'm so sorry about your wife.' She had never called Lola by name—it had always been 'your wife'.

'Thank you,' I said, and in the same breath added, 'I've missed you.'

Ana looked down at her basket. 'The avocados are a bargain today,' she said. 'Two big ones for a dollar.'

'I mean it,' I said again. 'I've missed you.'

A woman by the tomatoes was listening to our conversation, but I couldn't care less.

'Evan,' Ana said, putting down her basket and looking me in the eye. 'Your wife's dead.' She moved into the check-out queue. 'Have some respect.'

And that was the last time we met.

I arrange it for a Tuesday. Somehow it seems right to keep it to a Tuesday, for the sake of a short-lived tradition, or even as a little snub to Marcel. We organise it all through text messages, not the most romantic of mediums—not that this is a romantic meeting anyway—but she does finish her messages with a *D* for Daniella and a single *X* for a kiss.

On my way home from the shops, I buy a bouquet of tulips, a mix of red and orange ones. On my first date with Lola I'd bought her tulips. 'They're yellow,' I'd said, 'for friendship.' I was testing the water. When she looked dismayed, I was delighted. At home, I search the cupboards for a vase. I find the antique one my mother-in-law gave us for a wedding present. I trim the stems and fill the vase with water. The blooms bring some much needed colour to the hallway, but something about their bowed heads makes me sad.

It's Monday night, and Bea has invited me for dinner. Her home is a rented one-bedroom apartment in Northcote, which she and Edwina have made their own with a carefully selected collection of Edwina's artworks. One piece in particular looms over the tiny space, a large painting of an Asian woman with a distorted face. She watches me as I move around the room. When I go to the kitchen, it's partly to get away from her.

'Smells good,' I say.

'Moroccan tagine,' Bea replies, and lifts the lid on the clay pot. 'I've only done it once before. It was delicious.' In the past few months she's put on a few kilos, but it suits her. It softens her face.

'Where's Edwina?'

'At some artists' workshop in the country.'

'Tonight's the first time I've seen her paintings,' I say. 'She's talented.'

'I know.' Bea smiles proudly.

'Can I help with something?'

'No,' she says, throwing down her tea towel. She opens a

bottle of wine. 'Now it's just a matter of waiting.' She ushers me back into the living room. When I sit down on the couch I can feel the Asian woman's huge black eyes burning through the back of my head.

'So,' Bea says as she pours me a glass of wine. 'Edwina told me you stopped going to the life drawing class.'

'It's been a while. Months.'

'I thought you enjoyed it.'

'I did.'

'Then why did you stop?'

She always asks so many questions.

'I don't know, Bea,' I sigh. 'Can't we just drop it?'

'Okay.'

I take a sip of the wine. 'Where's this from?'

'Do you like it? House-warming gift from a friend.'

'It's very...' I look for the right words. 'Easy to drink.'

'Oh, that's what I was going to tell you,' Bea says. 'Did you see the paper today?'

'No. Why?'

She takes a newspaper from the magazine rack near the couch. 'In the obituaries,' she begins. 'Ana Hrustanovic from Pascoe Vale.'

At the mere mention of her name I feel sick. Bea passes me the paper. It's open at the death notices. Ana's name is circled in blue biro. I can barely concentrate enough to read the small print.

Ana Hrustanovic
13 September 1950–30 July 2009
Beloved mother of Adrijan and Damir.
You will always be in our hearts.

'Why are you showing me this?' I ask.

'Weren't you close to her?'

I search Bea's eyes for malice, but I don't find any. 'I don't know why you're doing this.'

'I thought you'd want to know. She was someone you were close to, a long time ago.'

'I never meant it, okay? It was stupid. I know. I ruined everything.'

'Dad.' Bea puts her glass down on the coffee table and places a hand on my knee. 'I might not have understood when I was fifteen, but I understand now.'

I can't believe this is happening. Can Lola see all of this?

'Please, let's not…'

'I've cheated on my girlfriends.'

'Please, Bea, I don't want to hear it.'

'I know what it's like. You don't think. Until it's all over, and it's too late.'

'Please.'

The timer on the oven goes off. Bea looks at the kitchen door and then turns back to look at me. She stares at me for what seems like an eternity, but I keep my gaze fixed on a stain on the carpet. Finally she gets up and goes into the kitchen. I can breathe again.

Today's the day. I wake up early and can't get back to sleep. As I pull on my robe and walk to the kitchen I'm pleased to see the house is spotless. I almost expect to find Lola at the stove, making me a cooked breakfast of bacon and eggs. She's not, but the eggs I cook are beautiful and creamy anyway.

I make the bed, pulling the sheets tight until every crease has been pressed out. I shave and put on a pair of jeans and a jumper. When I look in the mirror, I see the face of an old man, but an old man with promise in the curl of his old lips. I lug my easel from room to room and from corner to corner, searching for the perfect backdrop for my yet-to-be-conceived masterpiece. I imagine Daniella's long legs stretched across the old chaise longue in the sitting room. I picture her naked, leaning casually against the marble mantelpiece in the bedroom. I see her staring through the front window at the now bare arms of the Japanese maple.

At midday I walk to the milk bar and buy a packet of Winfields from the Chinese man. He is a man of few words—of no-frills Chinese efficiency—and today it's a relief, because I'm not in the mood for mindless chitchat. On the way home I smoke my first cigarette in thirty long, tobacco-free years. It feels good, comforting, like catching up with an old friend. I walk. I smoke. I walk and smoke.

I follow Glenlyon Road. I stroll past the gym-goers at the Brunswick Baths and the looming face of the Brunswick Town Hall. I pass the Brunswick Community Health Centre and the Shell petrol station on Lygon Street. Soon I know where I'm headed.

Merri Creek. The powerlines are the only reminder that I'm five kilometres from the city. If my hearing was better, I might be able to catch the rumble of a faraway tram, but mostly the air is full of birdsong. I remember bringing Bea here when she was a little girl, in spring, to feed the ducklings.

I cross the bridge, ignoring a boy spraying spiky words across its underbelly, and find a quiet spot on the opposite bank. I can't help but think about Lola and her faceless lover. Was this their spot? What did they do once they had settled into the dewy grass? Did they hold hands and recite poetry to each other in the dappled sunlight? Or did they tear off each other's clothes and fornicate in the grass?

It's peaceful here. I lie down, close my eyes and let the shadows of the leaves run back and forth across my face. The cigarettes have had their way with me. I surrender to the moment.

She's late. We said three-thirty and it's already ten to four. For the past hour I haven't been able to do anything except stare at the face of the clock. I don't know her, or what she likes. There's half a litre of Diet Coke in the fridge, an open bottle of red on the bench, a packet of Tim Tams in case she gets a craving, and cheese crackers if she prefers a bit of salt. I put my hand in my pocket and the cold metal of the cigarette lighter between my fingers calms me. If there's one thing I'm sure of, it's that she'll want a smoke.

At two minutes past four the doorbell rings, and my heart pounds against my ribs. Here she is, I think—not just a bunch of lines on a piece of paper, but the real thing, soft and warm and fleshy, in my hallway, my house. It's a moment to savour. I take a deep breath.

'Welcome,' I say, but it feels wrong, too formal.

She looks at me, her face unreadable, as she takes a long last drag of her cigarette. 'Thanks.'

She hangs her coat on the hatstand and loiters in front of an oil painting in the hallway—a generic Australian landscape, all orange and grey, with a few scattered gum trees.

'A gift,' I explain, and she nods. 'Not sure who the artist is.'

Silently she follows me into the front room. I've started a fire, and it's almost cosy. I'm pleased to see her relax a little. I pass her the one-dollar ashtray I picked up at the Brotherhood yesterday. 'You can smoke in here if you like,' I say, and I see her relax a little bit more. She shakes out another cigarette.

'Can I get you a drink of something?'

'I'd love a scotch.'

'I've got a bottle of red open?'

'That'll do.'

When I return, she's staring out the front window. Smoke is rising in soft tendrils from her cigarette. She takes a wineglass from my hand and rests it on the windowsill. 'Great house,' she says. 'You here by yourself?'

'Yes.' I take a sip of my wine.

'Must get pretty lonely,' she says and draws a line through the fog on the window. Her nails are chewed to the quick. 'Old houses freak me out a little. Bumps in the middle of the night.'

'I know all her noises,' I say, lighting a cigarette for myself.

'I've only ever lived in the family shithole and a bunch of student share houses.' She taps some ash into the ashtray. 'I'm just thankful when the roof's stuck on and nobody's used up the hot water.'

I grunt empathically.

'So,' she says, stubbing out her cigarette. 'Shall we do this?'

I'm glad she is the one to say it, not me.

'You *are* paying me by the hour, after all.'

I offer to leave the room while she undresses. 'Here,' I say, passing her Lola's kimono, a gift from one of her Japanese students. 'You can wear this.'

'Thanks,' she says and takes it from my hand.

I wait outside, imagining her eyeing the kimono,

smelling it—wondering who it belongs to, why it stinks of mothballs—and then unzipping her boots, sitting down to take off her socks, pulling her jeans off…

A photo of Lola on the hallway table catches my eye. I must have walked past it a thousand times before, but I've never really looked at it. I pick it up and look at it now. Lola is running away from the camera—she would have been a few weeks pregnant with Bea at the time—but her head is turned. For once her blond hair is loose and free, and she's laughing. Really laughing.

Daniella pokes her head through the doorway, holding the kimono tight around her neck. 'I'm ready,' she says. I go in again and stand by the easel at the window.

'Where do you want me?' she asks.

'You'd probably be most comfortable near the fire.'

'What about on the lounge?'

'If that suits you.'

Silently she moves to the chaise longue and slips out of the kimono. Her shoulders slouch and her hands gather around the triangle of hair between her legs. She lies down, her skin luminous against the red velvet of the chair. She rests her head on the nest of her arms and places her pink feet on the tufted cushion.

It's luxurious to have her here, all to myself. I pick up my pencil and draw. I start with her shoulder and follow the arch of her back down to her waist and then up again along the rise of her buttock. I sketch her breasts falling limply down, and her eyes looking up and out through the window. Time passes. Daylight surrenders to the warm glow of the table lamps. Shadows settle on the page like ashen moths.

'Evan?'

'Hmmm?' I murmur.

'I've got a cramp.'

I hold up my hand. 'Can you keep still for one more minute, please, Lola?'

'Lola?' she says.

At the mention of Lola's name I lose all concentration. 'Sorry?'

'Who's Lola?'

'Lola's my wife.' I put down my pencil. 'Ex-wife. I mean, not ex-wife. She's dead. But how did you—'

Suddenly Daniella is sitting up and the pose—and all hope for my drawing—is lost. 'Was this hers?' she screams, throwing the kimono across the room. 'My boyfriend was right. This is fucked up!'

'Daniella,' I say, trying to stay calm. 'What's the matter? What's happened?'

'Don't you realise? You called me by her name.' She spits as she speaks. 'You called me by your dead wife's fucking name!'

I feel my insides churn and spasm.

'Did she pose for you too?' she says, pulling on her jumper.

I plead for her to stay, but when I see her tear her coat from the hatstand I know she's made up her mind. It's over.

'At least let me pay you for your time.' I hold out two crisp fifty-dollar bills. She looks at them, and for a moment I think she will refuse, but then she rips them from my fingers. She walks through the front door and slams it as hard as she can in my face.

I go back to the front room and look around at the butts in the ashtray and the kimono on the floor with its arms outstretched. I can just see the trace of her lipstick on the rim of the half-empty wineglass.

Everything is white. I can't escape it, this whiteness. White walls, white-tiled floors and a white waffle blanket with a blue trim draped across my withered legs. They feel weird, my legs. I can't move one of them. I must be in a hospital, I think. I spent the last six months of Lola's life going in and out of hospitals.

I look around. There's a white bundle across the aisle, but it's hard to tell if it's just a couple of pillows or a living, breathing human being. A drip hangs from my arm, and on the board above my bed is written: NIL BY MOUTH.

'Well, well, well...' a nurse says as she enters the room. She drags an intravenous pole behind her. 'Wakey, wakey, sleepyhead!' I go to speak, but all that comes out is a grunt, and it's louder than I had intended. 'Be with you soon, Mr

Bailey,' the nurse calls from the other side of the room. She hooks a bag of fluid up to the white bundle across the aisle.

I must have had a stroke. It's the only explanation I can find for why half of my body feels like a lead weight, like it doesn't belong to me anymore. The nurse looks at me from the end of the bed. She is plump in a reassuring way and has a lanyard around her neck that tells me she is the nurse unit manager and her name is Cheryl. 'Mr Bailey,' she says, smiling. 'We've been waiting for you to wake up.'

We? Who's we?

'Your daughter, Bea, has been in here every day. She stays for as long as visiting hours will allow.'

Bea, of course. Forgiving Bea. There is a wetness on my cheek. Is it blood? Am I bleeding?

'Don't cry, Mr Bailey—she'll be here soon. Now, lift up your gown for me, there's a good man, and we'll give you your injection.'

I can only see glimpses of Bea's face through the bouquet of yellow tulips she holds in front of her.

'I couldn't bring you chocolates,' she says. 'You're being fed through a drip in your arm.' Behind the flowers she looks awful. Her eyes are raw from crying and her face is full of pimples.

I try to say something—something comforting—but the words refuse to come. Instead, she reassures me. 'Don't worry, Dad. Today's scans were looking better.' She holds my hand. 'Now it's time to rest.'

It's not so bad, having all these people fuss over me. At first I fought it, but that was partly for show, because I know I can't do it alone. The days begin with a shower. I can just about stand now, but in the shower I have to sit on a plastic stool as Cheryl waves the showerhead over me like a wand. Cheryl tells me what to do. She tells me when I need to stand, and when I need to stretch my arm to take the sleeve of my robe.

Breakfast is next. I have a bowl of porridge and a mouthful of canned peaches. I watch the *Today* show on the telly—a tiny one that Bea pays a ridiculous daily rate for— and sometimes I make small talk with Giuseppe across the aisle (who wasn't a pile of pillows after all).

Mostly, I enjoy being touched. I can't remember the last time someone touched me. Now I have Cheryl, who dresses me and moves my legs into a respectable position on the bed, and Bea, who combs my hair and shaves my shabby beard. Even Edwina kisses me on the forehead and pats me on the knee. It's through their hands that I'm healing.

It is my second week in hospital and Bea is sitting in the chair beside my bed, playing on her computer.

'How did you find me?' I say.

She looks up from the screen.

'I want to know.'

Bea closes the lid of her laptop. 'You were lying unconscious on the floor.'

'How long had I been there?'

'Hard to say. The fire in the grate was out, and your body temperature had dropped by the time the ambos arrived.'

I nod.

'I feel terrible I didn't find you sooner.'

'Don't be stupid. How were you to know? And what does it matter now anyway?'

'Yeah, well…The physio seems pretty happy with you today. He seems to think you'll make a full recovery.'

'That's what he says,' I say, but I think she senses my scepticism. 'Have you told Dr Jay?'

'He's been away. I spoke to him last night.'

'What did he say?'

'That he was sorry.'

'Not *I told you so*?'

'Dr Jay's not like that, Dad,' Bea says and rubs her eyes. She still looks tired. Woefully tired.

'All doctors are the same.'

'What's that supposed to mean?'

'You know how they are. We've got enough in the family to know.'

Bea sighs. 'You can't lump them all in the same class

as Grandpa, Dad.' She picks up an old magazine from my bedside table. 'Grandpa was a bastard.'

And just like that, in one fell swoop, she lops off the professor's head.

Lola died on a Wednesday. I was standing on the front verandah, watching hot air balloons and waiting for Dr Jay.

'Dad.'

I turned around to see Bea, in her pyjamas, clutching a mug of Milo. She'd pulled down the sleeves of her pyjama top to cover her blue and trembling hands.

'She's not looking too good.'

She's dying. Your mother's dying.

'I know,' I said, swallowing my tears and turning back to the floating balloons.

'Dad?' she said again, but this time she put a cold hand on my forearm. I see now that this was a plea—a plea for me, her father, to do something. To just fucking do something. And I still can't explain why, at this pivotal moment, I didn't show my daughter some compassion. Why didn't I take her hand in mine? Why didn't I pull her into my embrace? Why was it so impossible for me to shake the guilt I felt when I saw her beseeching face?

'I'd better go in,' I said. Bea let go of my arm, but for a long time I could still feel the touch of her cold fingers on my skin.

*

It is my fourth week in rehab. It's nearly five and the light is beginning to wane. Lisa, the kitchen lady, will be round with dinner soon, and she'll give me two bread rolls because she likes me.

'Dad?'

'Hmmm?' I open my eyes.

'They're talking about discharging you.'

I nod.

'How do you feel about going home?'

I'm petrified.

'Okay,' I say.

Bea looks at the *Who* magazine in her lap. She flicks through the pages without interest. I can smell the trolley of food coming down the corridor and my mouth is flushed with saliva.

'How would you feel,' she asks, 'about me and Edwina moving in?'

I'd feel guilty, horribly guilty.

'You don't have to do that. You've both got your own lives,' I say.

'But what if we wanted to?'

I look at the television. Some old man with a posh accent is telling an excited woman her vase is worth two hundred pounds. 'And Edwina?' I ask.

'It was her idea.'

Why wasn't it your idea?

'It'll be good for all of us. We'll save on rent,' she says. 'Not to mention we could do with the extra room.' She looks at me expectantly, but I don't know what else to say. I keep watching the television.

'In case you haven't noticed, I'm pregnant,' Bea says. I must look confused, because she quickly adds, 'Sperm donor.'

Say something. Don't just sit there like a stunned mullet.

'Congratulations.'

Bea smiles. For once I've said the right thing.

'And Dad?' she says, rubbing her swollen tummy, her pregnancy suddenly apparent. 'It's a boy.'

I turn off the television.

'That's great, Bea. Really great.'

A knot is forming in my throat.

'And he's going to need a man in his life.'

The tears are streaming from my eyes.

'Don't cry.'

But I can't stop, because I know what it means. I've wanted it for so long—a second chance.

The house is full of fresh flowers. Edwina's paintings adorn the walls. The fridge is packed with exotic cheeses and homemade pesto and jams. The rooms look lived in, with undies and socks strewn across their floors.

It's summer and the days are long and hot. Bea and I take

evening walks and, with her heavy belly and my bad leg, we fall into a comfortable pace. Today I lead her along Glenlyon Road and down towards Merri Creek. We sit by the water. I feed the ducks. Bea talks about how sick and tired she is of being pregnant. Her fat ankles stick out beneath her skirt. I smile at her. She closes her eyes and lets the sun warm her face.

I never believed it could be this way.

It's the middle of the night. I look at the clock. Two-thirty. I can hear their feet on the creaking floorboards. I can hear their whispers on the stairs.

'Evan?'

I sit straight up in bed.

'What? What's happening?'

'I'm taking Bea to the hospital,' Edwina says. 'Her water just broke.'

I jump out of bed and nearly trip over my cane, which has fallen to the floor. Edwina switches on the light.

'You don't need to come,' she says, helping me up.

'I'm coming,' I say, and something in my voice must be convincing, because she doesn't protest again.

'Slow down,' Bea says between breaths as we speed down Royal Parade.

'Does it hurt?' I ask.

There is fire in her eyes. 'Of course it fucking hurts!'

There's an awkward silence before Edwina and I laugh and even Bea breaks into a sideways smile. There's no traffic at this time of the morning and we get to the hospital within minutes.

I escort Bea inside while Edwina parks the car. She leans on me and I lean on my cane. I can't help but think what an odd pair we must make as we go through the sliding doors. I lead Bea towards a sign that reads *Triage*.

'Excuse me,' I say to the nurse at the desk. 'My daughter's about to have a baby.'

I expect her to say congratulations and send someone to wheel Bea straight up to the ward. Instead she shuffles some papers on her desk and passes a blue form to us through the window.

'Fill this out,' she says.

Bea and I retreat to the plastic seats in the waiting room. I've forgotten my glasses and I'm useless to her, but soon Edwina arrives and takes control.

She's good for us, I think. Like glue.

I don't remember much about when Bea was born. Back in those days, men weren't allowed into the delivery suite. All I have is a hazy memory of sitting outside and chain-smoking until the nurse finally called me in.

It's cold in the waiting room. I balance a plastic cup of

instant coffee on my tremulous legs. I look at the clock: five am. Another man and his two kids are getting drinks from the vending machine. I try not to imagine what's going on upstairs. Every so often an image flashes before my eyes: Bea, hair plastered to her forehead, with Edwina holding her sweaty hand. A black head. A rush of air. A cry. Or worse, Bea being wheeled through double doors.

I must have fallen asleep. A man taps me on the shoulder. He's one of the cleaners, and he has arrived to mop away the evening's grime.

'What time is it?' I ask groggily, sitting up.

'Six o'clock.'

The cleaner is a big man. He could just as well have made a career as a bodyguard. 'You waiting for something?' he asks.

'A little boy.'

He raises his eyebrows. 'You the father?'

'God, no. I'm almost seventy years old.'

'You never know. I see everything here. All kinds of families. Families you could never imagine.'

I think of Bea and Edwina. Two mothers.

'Do you have children of your own?' I ask, snatching a look at his name tag, which reads *Drago*.

Drago looks around the lobby and, seeing that the coast is clear, takes a seat next to me. 'I have three children and one grandchild,' he says, and pulls a tattered photo from his wallet. Three pairs of smiling brown eyes.

'Beautiful,' I say.

And that's how Edwina finds me, with another man's family in my hands.

She has tears in her eyes.

'He's here.'

I don't say anything to Edwina. I don't want to spoil it. I don't want to hear anything until I see his little face. I want to see his face first, and then hers. That's how I'll know everything's okay.

At first he's just a wriggling bundle of flesh in her arms. Like the shapeless white mound that Giuseppe—now my friend—used to be. But as she unwraps his head to reveal his scrunched-up little face, I see that he is all me. Poor bugger.

'Take him,' Bea says, holding him out to me like a gift.

'I can't,' I say and point to my cane. 'I'll drop him.'

Edwina drags a chair from by the window and pushes it next to the bed. She takes my cane and points to the chair. I sit down as I am told.

'Meet your grandson,' Bea says, and I open my arms to receive him. 'Sebastian Evan Bailey.' And suddenly he's in my arms, blinking and looking everywhere and nowhere all at once. His skin is warm and pink and covered in a feathery white down. I bury my nose in the folds of his flesh. I breathe him in. Now this, I think to myself, this I remember.

*

He adores me. When others say it I deny it, but I know that it's true. And I've done nothing to deserve it. Except love him, which is easy. He's not like Bea. When Bea was little she was hard work. She was stubborn, inflexible, strong. If anything, Sebastian is too sensitive, too quick to cry, too fragile. He's always getting sick and having fevers.

Motherhood has been good to Bea. It's calmed her. For a while it even helped her relationship with Edwina. But recently things have taken a turn for the worse. I can hear the late-night arguments through my bedroom wall. Hushed accusations followed by long, weighty silences. I don't interfere. Except to take Sebastian away and give them some time alone.

Today we're at Merri Creek and Sebastian is chasing a butterfly. He's running in circles, following the winged creature from branch to branch, flower to flower. I lay a blanket on the grass and get down on my knees.

'Pa?' Sebastian says, bored with the butterfly.

'Yes?'

'Are you married?'

I smile. I can never predict what will come out of his little mouth.

'Used to be.'

He plays with a pair of ladybirds in the grass.

'Who are you married to?' he says, looking up at me.

'I'm married to your grandma,' I say. 'Grandma Lola.'

'Grandma Lola.'

A jogger runs past us, his German shepherd in tow. They pant loudly and in unison.

'I'm thirsty,' says Sebastian.

I reach into the bag Bea has packed for us and, sure enough, there is a box of Ribena—Sebastian's favourite—inside. He takes the first few sips thirstily.

'Pa?'

'Yes, my cheeky monkey?'

He laughs. I love to see him laugh.

'What was Grandma Lola like?'

I think of her. I think of her perfect white skin and her pale blond hair. I think of her sitting by the fire in the front room of our house, lost in one of her books. I think back to the photo in the hallway—a moment of freedom, her hair loose and flying, her soft mouth stretched into a smile.

'You know the butterfly you were chasing before?'

'Yep,' Sebastian says, and nods his head vigorously.

'Your Grandma Lola was like that.'

'She was beautiful like the butterfly,' he says. It is not a question but a statement. I look down at the two ladybirds fornicating in the grass.

'Yes. So very beautiful.' But he's gone. Disappeared into the bushes, chasing another butterfly.

*

When we get home the air is thick with the smell of melted butter. In the kitchen, chocolate chip biscuits cool on a wire rack above the stovetop. Sebastian climbs onto a stool, dips his finger into a mixing bowl. The radio is on, but Bea is nowhere to be seen. I give one of the biscuits to Sebastian and go in search of his mother. I find her, asleep in her bedroom, still wearing her chocolate-smeared apron. Sebastian tries to wake her, but I pull him away, tell him to finish his biscuit. There is a suitcase in the corner of the room, half-packed with Edwina's clothes and art history books. I lift Bea's foot, heavy with sleep, and place it with her other foot on the mattress. I motion to Sebastian to help me and together we pick a sheet off the floor and tuck it around Bea's body.

They framed her. Now she sits, in thick unpolished wood, above the marble mantelpiece in my bedroom. I objected at first, insisting she wasn't worth the money, but in truth I was pleased with the finished piece. She looked good. Bea and Edwina kept saying I could sell her, and probably for a good price, too, but I could never part with her. I think even Bea knew that.

I try not to think back to that day. I try not to remember the disgust smeared across Daniella's otherwise lovely face. I force myself to forget the red ladder of lines on the soft belly of her arm. Daniella. I never even knew her real name.

Nowadays, when I look at the drawing, it's not Daniella I see at all. It's Lola. It can't possibly be anyone else, with that long arched neck and easy elegance. And there, too, in the drawing, is Ana—lovely Ana—in the wide, munificent hips. But it's also Bea. In the wistful, other-worldly eyes. Eyes that no longer accuse me of crimes past, or crimes yet to be committed. Tender eyes. Soft. Like they used to be when she was little. Like they are becoming again now.

A Good and Pleasant Thing

Twenty years ago supermarkets didn't stock Chinese mushrooms. Now they had a whole aisle dedicated to international cuisine. Lebanese, Greek and Mexican on one side, Chinese, Vietnamese and Indian on the other. Mrs Chan hardly ever went to the shops by herself. On Wednesdays her eldest daughter, Lily, took her to Footscray Market to buy fresh vegetables, and every Friday her youngest daughter, Daisy, ordered bulky items, like toilet paper, for her online. But today was her grandson Martin's twentieth birthday, and Mrs Chan wanted to surprise him—to surprise all of them—by cooking a family favourite. Chinese clay pot chicken and mushroom rice.

She found the chicken thighs towards the front of the

supermarket, cradled in polystyrene. The meat would be days old by now, but it would have to do. In Hong Kong, Mrs Chan would have sent her maid to choose a live chicken at Wan Chai Market and pick it up an hour later—dead, plucked and washed. When the Chan family feasted on the flesh for dinner, the meat would be less than six hours old. That was why the meals Mrs Chan made in Australia would always be poor imitations—bland and watery substitutes for their Hong Kong originals. But today she was heartened by the plumpness of the ginger and the crispness of the spring onions, and on finding a familiar brand of dried Chinese mushrooms she was eager to start cooking.

It was only once she was waiting in line that Mrs Chan noticed the Australian flags hanging from the ceiling. As she looked around, she realised the entire store was decorated with green and gold balloons. Now she remembered her grandson shared his birthday with an Australian holiday.

When Mrs Chan reached the front of the queue, the pretty girl behind the counter in the yellow headscarf smiled and said something in English. Mrs Chan shook her head and said 'No fly buys!' like her daughter Lily had trained her to do. The girl seemed amused by this, and Mrs Chan wondered if perhaps she had asked her something else. She would never know.

As she watched her items being scanned and bagged, Mrs Chan turned her attention to the magazine rack. A sea of women with pouty lips and cascading hair returned her stare. They reminded Mrs Chan of the Barbies her granddaughter had played with as a child. Once, long ago, Mrs Chan had been the local bombshell. But that was in the 1960s, and hers had been a real, unspoilt kind of beauty. Her fair skin and high cheekbones had caused a stir among the neighbours, some of the more jealous ones starting a rumour she had Caucasian blood in her.

There was only one face Mrs Chan recognised amid all the others on the covers of the glossy magazines— a woman with cumquat-coloured hair. When Mrs Chan had first come to Australia, the red-headed woman had been outspoken about Chinese migrants, but thankfully nobody, including the redhead, talked about the Chinese anymore. Now it was all about Muslims—like the pretty girl in the yellow headscarf scanning Mrs Chan's Chinese mushrooms.

Not one person offered Mrs Chan a seat on the tram. She was too short to reach the plastic hand-straps and clung to a pole near the door instead. Every so often she glared at the teenager slumped in the seat reserved for disabled people, but the pimply boy was plugged into his phone, oblivious to everything.

When she arrived home, Mrs Chan soaked the mushrooms. She watched their parched black heads grow round and plump in the warm water. She washed the rice and chopped up all the ingredients. It wasn't long before the air in the kitchen was thick with the smell of ginger and spring onion. Her mobile rang just as she was unwrapping her precious clay pot—the one she had brought to Australia, cocooned in bubble wrap, in her hand luggage.

'Hello?'

'Celestial Gardens. Tonight. Six o'clock. For Martin's birthday.' Lily, a bank manager, had inherited this punchy way of talking from her father. Wei had been an accountant—full of stress, dead at fifty-three from a heart attack.

'I thought you'd come here, to my house. Like every Sunday.'

'It's Martin's birthday, Ma. He's twenty. He doesn't want to go to his poh poh's house for dinner.'

'You could have told me earlier.'

'I would have…but I thought you'd forget.'

'I'm cooking Martin's favourite. Clay pot chicken rice.'

'I've booked Celestial Gardens. Paid a deposit and everything.'

Mrs Chan looked at the mushrooms, floating now, in liquid the colour of dishwater. She couldn't argue with a deposit.

'Besides,' Lily said, 'it's thirty-three degrees. Not clay pot weather.'

*

Celestial Gardens was on the first floor of a building in Chinatown. A glass box perched above a Chinese bakery and a registered Apple reseller. It was popular for its dumplings, but Mrs Chan hated it. There were better, more authentic places in suburbs like Box Hill and Doncaster. But Martin had recently moved to the city, to an apartment bought by his mother, and the restaurant was convenient for him. He was going to a bar with his friends after dinner.

Mrs Chan arrived with her youngest daughter. Daisy was in her early forties and a successful lawyer. In the car she spoke endlessly about a case she had taken on, some high-profile international child custody battle. There had been a current affairs program about it and everything. While proud of her daughter's success, Mrs Chan didn't delight in what Daisy did for a living, which was basically profiting, very well, from the failure of marriages. For Mrs Chan, marriage was forever, no matter how excruciating. And she blamed Daisy's job for her lack of suitors. Because what man in his right mind would want to marry a divorce lawyer?

Mrs Chan stared through her window as squat weatherboard houses gave way to shiny office towers. It was here in the city that Mrs Chan felt most at home, swaddled by lights and strangers and traffic noise. But there was something underwhelming about the Melbourne CBD— dull and unimaginative compared to the glittering metropolis of Hong Kong.

At the restaurant Mrs Chan got lost amid a flurry of kisses. She found an empty chair in the corner near a potted plant and collapsed into it. She couldn't remember exactly when this silly kissing business had begun. The grandchildren had started doing it with their Australian friends, and then one day everybody in the family was joining in. It made Mrs Chan uncomfortable, panicky even. She was always leaning in the wrong way and knocking cheekbones with somebody.

As a young woman, Mrs Chan would never have imagined she and her family would end up in Australia. She knew nothing about the country, other than that it was once a British colony, like Hong Kong. But then all of a sudden, in the nineties, everybody in Hong Kong was moving to Canada and Australia, nervous about the end of British rule. It made sense for Mr and Mrs Chan to send their children to university in Melbourne.

From her seat in the corner, Mrs Chan watched her family. There was Lily, hovering around everybody, watching everything. A neurotic creature from birth, Lily had always slept and eaten very little. She grew from a thin, perfectionist child into a thin, perfectionist adult. It was Lily who reminded them all about anniversaries, told them how much money to put in their red packets for Chinese New Year and organised large family gatherings like Martin's birthday dinner tonight. Lily enjoyed neatness and order and punctuality. That was why Mrs Chan was so surprised when she had married Luke—a balding, pot-bellied English teacher who had been trying to write a screenplay for fifteen years. Mrs Chan didn't like him—she had the impression he held her daughter back. Luke started things, Lily finished them. Lily made money, Luke spent it. When Luke drifted, Lily steered him back on course. Fortunately Martin took after his mother—despite spending an inordinate amount of time with his chaotic father. Like Lily, Martin was frighteningly intelligent and unforgivingly precise. He could do no wrong in Mrs Chan's eyes.

She observed her grandson now. He was smiling and accepting red packets of money. Unlike other boys his age, Martin did not slouch. He held his head high and towered above the rest of the family. Mrs Chan planned on leaving him everything in her will. Martin was her one and only grandson. Rose, her middle child, had already had twelve unsuccessful cycles of IVF, and Daisy was too happy being single to get married. There was a granddaughter in Sydney, too—Martin's older sister—but she had a tattoo and was probably in a relationship with a woman, and nobody ever mentioned her.

Rose was chatting to Martin, blushing and laughing and covering her hand with her mouth. She was the quiet one of the bunch. When she was born, the midwife said she had an old man's face, serious and watchful. She never crawled—instead, for months, Rose had studied Lily running rings around her mother, and then one morning, around her first birthday, she simply stood up and walked. Rose was the smartest of the three girls, but from a young age she had learnt to defer to her bossy sister Lily. Mrs Chan knew that behind her daughter's solemn look lurked a profound insecurity. Rose had chosen to study pharmacy at university even though her marks were high enough to get into medicine. Soon after graduation she had married David, a plastic surgeon—also from Hong Kong—who offered family discounts for breast implants and answered his phone in the middle of dinner.

Daisy, the youngest daughter, was the most easygoing. From two weeks of age, she had slept for twelve hours straight every night. Daisy fit into Australia better than the rest of them, saying whatever came into her head and swearing like an Aussie. Mrs Chan watched her now, making her way around the room, telling self-deprecating stories and making everybody laugh.

Mrs Chan wondered what her husband would think of his daughters if he were alive. No doubt he would be proud. He had only lived long enough to see Lily and Rose finish university. When the girls were growing up, Wei never hid the fact that what he'd really wanted was a son. Mrs Chan could see now that this had only spurred his daughters on.

She watched Martin excuse himself from the group and navigate between the tables towards her. Her grandson spoke very basic and halting Cantonese. Mrs Chan had spoken it to him as a baby, but when he was older, Martin had always insisted on answering her in English. Nowadays she couldn't have anything more than a simple conversation with him. But she loved him. She loved how handsome he was. She loved that he had both the double-lidded eyes of his father and the smooth, flawless skin of his mother. He pulled up a chair and sat down beside her. In his funny Cantonese, he thanked her for her gift—a red packet containing two hundred Australian dollars. Mrs Chan waved her hand and smiled and mumbled that it was nothing. He patted her awkwardly on the shoulder.

Lily yelled at them all to sit down and eat. Martin left his grandmother to join his parents on the other side of the table. The food was ordinary. The pork crackling was chewy, the broccoli was cold and the rice was overcooked. When the meal was finished, Mrs Chan pulled a toothpick from a tiny vase on the lazy Susan and hid her mouth with her hand as she retrieved some broccoli from between her teeth. As always, the plastic surgeon was fiddling with his phone. Daisy was dominating the talk, dipping in and out of Cantonese. Mrs Chan could only catch snippets of the conversation.

'I wouldn't care if it was on a different day...or called a different thing...so long as we get a public holiday!'

Lily jumped in then with something in English. Mrs Chan could sense a rift forming between her children.

Luke's red face was becoming redder. Lily was flapping her tiny hands. Mrs Chan was relieved when the plastic surgeon pushed back his chair and stood up.

'I'm sorry,' he said in needlessly loud Cantonese. 'I have to go. An old lady in a nursing home cut her face open.' He rolled his eyes. 'She's eighty-three.'

Minutes later Martin's phone rang. His friends were waiting for him downstairs. He said a hurried goodbye. After he had left, Mrs Chan watched him through the restaurant window. She saw him greet his friends. They bumped shoulders and smacked each other on the back. He was a different person with them, rough and masculine.

Without Martin, there was no point to the gathering. Lily asked for the bill. When it arrived, she and Daisy played tug of war with the docket while Rose stuffed thick wads of cash into her sisters' expensive handbags. Finally somebody won or somebody else conceded, as they always did, and they all waited by the lift while Rose and Lily went to the bathroom.

'Are you sure you don't need to use the toilet, Ma?' Daisy asked, as if talking to a three-year-old. Mrs Chan didn't want to give Daisy the satisfaction of being right, but she had drunk a lot of jasmine tea, and her bladder had a funny way of misbehaving lately. She slunk off towards the rest rooms.

Rose and Lily were still in the cubicles when Mrs Chan walked in. As she prepared the toilet seat with layers of paper, Mrs Chan heard the flush of the toilets, followed by the clicking of her daughters' heels as they walked to the handbasins.

'You know she won't be able to live in that unit forever,' Lily said in a low voice. Mrs Chan could barely catch her words over the sound of a tap running.

'I know,' Rose said, 'but I've been meaning to tell you, David's applied to Sydney next year for his fellowship.'

There was a pause.

'So you won't be around either.'

'I'm not sure.'

They switched to English then, but Daisy's name was mentioned once or twice in angry tones before their voices were drowned out by the whirr of the hand dryer.

On the car ride home, Daisy launched into her usual tirade about her sisters. Mrs Chan had heard it all before. Why did Rose put up with that arrogant prick of a doctor? Why did Lily spoil Martin so much? Why did they all have to go along with Lily's delusion that she was the glue that held the family together? Why didn't anybody ever point out that Lily had effectively disowned her own daughter? Every so often Mrs Chan nodded or grunted to show Daisy she was still listening, but really she was filling in the gaps in the conversation she had overheard in the toilet at the restaurant. She told herself she wasn't going to mention it to Daisy. She didn't want to contribute to any further conflict between her daughters. But when Daisy pulled up in front of her unit, Mrs Chan was bursting to say something. She couldn't face the thought of going inside to sit alone with those terrible words still spinning around in her head.

'Your sisters want to put me in a home,' she said. Mrs Chan knew this wasn't exactly what the girls had said, but she wanted to see her youngest daughter explode with indignation. She was shocked when Daisy leant her elbows on the steering wheel and rubbed her eyes.

'Lily and I had an understanding. We were going to talk to Rose first before we brought it up with you.'

Mrs Chan said nothing. She was trying to understand how her three very different daughters—women who fought about anything and everything—had managed to come to an agreement on this issue.

Daisy reached across her mother and opened the glove box. She pulled out a brochure and laid it on Mrs Chan's lap. At the top, in English and Chinese, it said: *Australia's Number One Chinese Retirement Village*. Below the heading was a quote from Confucius: *Old age, believe me, is a good and pleasant thing*. There was a photo on the front cover of brick-veneer houses with Chinese-style eaves. A pretty garden was framed with pink camellia and bamboo.

'I've checked it out,' Daisy said, staring straight ahead through the windscreen. 'It's beautiful.'

Mrs Chan huffed. She opened her door and stepped out

onto the street. For a moment she considered throwing the brochure back in her daughter's guilty face, but instead she settled for slamming the car door as hard as she could.

Lying in bed, Mrs Chan looked through the brochure. The Chinese translation described the home as a *deluxe facility*. In total, there were eight units, each with two bedrooms. The rooms were immaculate, with built-in alarms and shiny rails in the bathrooms. Basic cooking facilities were provided, but residents had the option of two cooked meals a day in the dining room. There were weekly tai chi classes and, more recently, art therapy. Mrs Chan searched the brochure for photos of the residents. She found two: one of a man in a wheelchair holding up a crude painting of himself, and the other of a woman with rosy cheeks blowing out candles on a birthday cake.

Mrs Chan had only been inside a nursing home once, to visit a family friend with multiple sclerosis. Lily had driven her. She remembered thinking it was like a hospital without the doctors and the frenzy. Her friend was curled beneath a waffle blanket. Other, more able-bodied residents sat in the lounge room with their eyes closed and their mouths open. Mrs Chan's clearest memory was of a fly landing on one woman's face and dancing across her eyelashes.

*

When she had first arrived in Melbourne, a year after Wei died, Mrs Chan had lived with Lily and her family. Rose and Daisy were sharing a tiny apartment in the city. Martin was just a few weeks old and his sister was three at the time. There was plenty to do and Mrs Chan had earned her keep, cooking and cleaning and babysitting. But when the kids got older and had lives of their own, everything changed. Without her grandchildren around to act as a buffer, the relationship between Mrs Chan and her son-in-law grew sour. Mrs Chan could see that her mere presence irritated Luke, like a mosquito humming in his ear. For a while she did her best to avoid him, spending the winter days reading Chinese newspapers beside a fan heater in her room. At night she retired early so Luke and Lily could watch those detective shows they liked so much. But deep down Mrs Chan knew her days were numbered.

It was a relief for everyone when Daisy bought Mrs Chan a small two-bedroom unit in Footscray. The building was three tram stops away from Lily and not too far from Daisy's townhouse in Yarraville. Her daughters paid for her to have a personal alarm—a pendant she wore on a chain around her neck with a button that alerted a response team—but even so the first few months were frightening. Mrs Chan had never lived by herself before. She had gone straight from her parents' tiny flat in Kowloon to her husband's spacious apartment on Hong Kong Island. The nine months of her first pregnancy had been quiet—weeks and weeks of watching her carefully prepared meals turn cold as she waited for Wei to return home—but then Lily had come along, followed by Rose, and finally Daisy, and Mrs Chan had never been lonely again. This new isolation took some getting used to. The silence in particular was unsettling—Australia was so quiet compared to Hong Kong. Eventually, though, she had adjusted. Mrs Chan was starting to believe she could get used to anything.

She woke up late the next morning in a tangle of sheets. The air conditioner had short-circuited again—as it always did when the temperature hit thirty degrees. The air was hot and still, like before a typhoon, except there were no typhoons in Melbourne. Mrs Chan wet a face towel with water from the tap and held the cloth to her forehead.

At midday, she put on a cotton dress and a wide-brimmed hat and went outside into the heat. Perhaps she would get an ice-cream. Dr Leung had said she was borderline diabetic, but one ice-cream wouldn't hurt. The doctor had been saying she was borderline diabetic for fifteen years. Mrs Chan was not a sweaty person, but as she walked she could feel a trickle of perspiration between her thighs. The streets were abandoned. Either side of her, fibro houses blinked and sagged in the sunlight. Hong Kong summers were different—sticky and wet and less intense. This kind of heat was extraordinary, as if Australia were closer to the sun.

What was normally a ten-minute walk to the shops seemed more like half an hour, and soon she stopped to rest in the shade of a small wattle tree. Mrs Chan took a sip from her bottle of water before pulling out the mobile phone her daughters had given her last year for her seventieth birthday. Martin had changed the settings to Chinese characters, and when her daughters called their faces appeared on the tiny screen as if by magic. But there were no messages or missed calls for Mrs Chan today. It must be thirty-five degrees and people her age were dying like insects from the heat, but none of her children seemed to care. That was the problem with Australia, she thought—so many old people left on their own. She had once heard about a woman found by police a whole week after she had died, her body half-devoured by her own starving pet dog. It made Mrs Chan furious. She stared at the empty message bank on her phone and decided to teach her daughters a lesson.

Just up the road was an old, run-down motel. Mrs Chan must have walked past it a hundred times, but she'd never taken much notice of it before. The building had water stains like black mascara running down its ugly concrete face. She hesitated in the driveway. When a neon bulb hissed above her head she almost aborted her plan, but then a neatly dressed Asian woman emerged from the foyer and Mrs Chan took this to be a good omen. She walked through the sliding doors and approached the surly girl at the desk. She held up her index finger and, in broken English, asked for a room. The girl didn't question the lack of luggage, or the hat, or the thongs. She just took the eighty dollars cash and flicked a battered key across the counter.

Mrs Chan regretted her decision as soon as she opened the door to the room. There was a funny odour—like the smell of damp towels left in the washing machine overnight. Mrs Chan inspected the bed. The mauve quilt had a cluster of mysterious grey stains near the middle. The pillow looked clean enough, but when she lifted it a long black hair fell from its belly. She found a towel in the bathroom and, after inspecting it carefully, laid it on the two-seater couch in the corner. She sat down, kicked off her thongs and hugged her knees to her chest. Her daughters would never think to look for her here. She would make them worry about her like she had always worried about them.

Somehow she dozed off, still sitting on the couch. When she woke, the alarm clock beside the bed told her it was two o'clock. She could feel a circular dent in her face where her cheek had rested on her knee. She checked her phone. Nothing. She turned on the TV. On one channel there were lots of women in bikinis with disproportionately large breasts. Mrs Chan watched for five minutes before a red message popped up on the screen. Scared that she had done something illegal, she turned off the television and sat in silence. She wondered if Wei had stayed at places like this when he travelled for work. She tried to imagine him walking through the door, loosening his tie and watching one of the big breast movies. They had been married for more than thirty years, but there was still so much she would never know about him.

When she'd first met Wei, he was already engaged to a girl from a good family. But Wei was a sucker for beauty— the rich girl never stood a chance. Mrs Chan lost her virginity on her wedding night as many women did in those days, but the way Wei unbuttoned her blouse and thrust his hands into her underwear suggested she was not his first, second or third. It would not have surprised Mrs Chan if Wei had watched the big breast movies. He must have been getting his excitement somewhere. In their last ten years of marriage he certainly hadn't been getting it from her—they went to bed at different times, often sleeping in separate rooms because of his snoring, but Mrs Chan knew urges like that didn't just disappear as people got older.

Her reverie was interrupted by a loud bang at the window. Terrified but also curious, she got up to peer out from behind the curtain. Just below the window she saw a man, about thirty perhaps, or a little older, lying on the ground. He must have collapsed and hit his head on the window on the way down. There was a cut on his forehead and a smear of blood on the glass. He wasn't moving. Mrs Chan's throat felt tight, as if it might close up at any moment. She held her trembling hands to her neck, forced herself to swallow. No one came running—she was the only person in the world who knew this man was injured, maybe even dying. She could probably save him by calling emergency, but she wouldn't be able to explain what had happened to the person at the other end of the line. Her other option was to drag the grumpy girl from reception to the wounded man at the back of the motel, but Mrs Chan was worried about implicating herself in the process. Wouldn't the authorities wonder what an old Chinese woman was doing alone in a seedy motel? Hadn't Daisy told her recently about some tourist being held in detention because she'd lost her wallet and couldn't speak English?

She returned to her spot on the couch and began gently rocking. What was it about rocking that human beings found so soothing? She remembered pressing baby Lily to her breasts in the early hours of the morning, not knowing how to stop her red-faced daughter from crying except by holding her as tight as she could and swaying her body back and forth in the darkness.

Mrs Chan didn't stop rocking until she heard the ambulance siren. Then she sat very still and watched the red light oscillating through the curtain. She heard a sharp metallic click, like a stretcher being unfolded. Mrs Chan hoped to God the man was still alive, that the paramedics hadn't come too late. In the hours after Wei's death, the doctors had told her it was because his heart had stopped so long before the ambulance arrived that he'd stood little chance of surviving.

After the ambulance had left, the ridiculousness of her situation dawned on her. Mrs Chan went to the bathroom and splashed some cold water across her face. Wary of using the towel hanging from the rail next to the sink, she wiped her hands on the skirt of her dress. She returned to the lounge and picked her straw hat up off the coffee table. Just as she was about to leave, her phone rang. Martin's handsome face flashed up on the small screen.

'Poh Poh? Where are you?' He was speaking Cantonese—Mrs Chan could only just understand him.

'Outside. In the garden.'

'Mum said you cooked chicken rice for my birthday.'

Martin. Dear, sweet Martin. Thank God for grandsons like Martin.

'I did.'

'Can I come over to eat it?'

Her heart soared. 'Of course.'

As Mrs Chan hung up, she thought of all the things she needed to do. She would have to soak a new bunch of mushrooms, slice the ginger and garlic, chop and marinate the chicken. She pulled the door closed behind her and returned the key to the grouchy girl at reception.

Martin was a good boy. Mrs Chan had known it from

the moment she held his tiny body during her first night in Melbourne. She knew it from the way he always took time to speak to her, softly, away from the others. She knew it from the warmth in his eyes as he stumbled over his Cantonese words. Mrs Chan put on her hat, took a deep breath and braced herself. She barely flinched as she stepped outside into the searing summer sun.

ACKNOWLEDGEMENTS

It gives me great pleasure to publicly thank the people who helped deliver this book into the world. First and foremost I must thank the Wheeler Centre and the judges of the 2016 Victorian Premier's Literary Award for an Unpublished Manuscript. Without the recognition of that very prestigious prize, my book would probably still be sitting at the bottom of a slush pile somewhere. Instead, I am supported by a group of wonderful professionals. Thank you to Clare Forster from Curtis Brown Australia, Michael Heyward and the team at Text for their faith in the manuscript, and my editor, Elizabeth Cowell, for her amazing ability to edit in a simultaneously ruthless and gentle way.

One of the best things I ever did was enrol in a writing course with Writers Victoria. That is where I met Mark Smith, a talented writer who has become a great friend and mentor. Mark taught me perseverance—an essential skill for any writer. He also stressed the importance of the rewrite, and over the years I have been lucky to find writer-friends like Daniel Harper and Keren Heenan to read and critique my work. Together they have helped to shape many of the stories in this collection. Mark, Daniel and Keren, thank you for your wisdom.

Some of the pieces in this collection have been published

elsewhere. 'Ticket-holder Number 5' and 'Muse' were first published in the *Griffith Review*, 'Things That Grow' appeared in *Sleepers Almanac*, 'Allomother' was published in the Bridport Prize anthology, 'White Sparrow' first appeared in *Shibboleth and Other Stories* and 'Clear Blue Seas' was featured in the Forty South anthology. I will always be grateful to these journals for the important work they do and for taking a chance on me and my writing.

I would like to conclude by acknowledging my family. Thank you, Mum and Dad, for reading everything I write. Without your support and generosity I would never have been able to pursue a career in writing. Thank you to my brother, Justin, my sister-in-law, Sonia, and my good friend Vicky for supporting me at various launches and writing events. Thank you, Dr Haissam Chahal, Ahed Chahal, Dana and Hani. I am indebted to you for your cooking and babysitting and for welcoming me into your culture and teaching me a great deal. Thank you, Rani. You thought you were marrying a doctor but ended up with a doctor-writer. You have taken it all in your stride and become a great champion for the book. This book, like our children, is a product of the life we have made together. Finally, thank you to Alyssa and Toby, who—while not always thrilled with my writing commitments—have roused emotions in me I never knew I possessed and in so doing have made me a crazier, more vulnerable and insightful human being.